KV-004-449

STORM OVER MENDARO

Brad Lando had ridden a hell-trail along the Mexican border — a loner with hard eyes and a reputation as a fast man with a gun. Now he wanted to end the trouble and violence which had followed him for more than three years, but in the tiny border town of Mendaro he rode into a nest of murder and intrigue that threatened to engulf the entire territory. The only law in Mendaro was that dealt out by a .45. Lando's only weapons were courage and his single pearl-handled Colt.

HAMPSHIRE COUNTY LIBRARY

F | 1 84395 258 0

CO13524139

JAMES ADAMS

STORM OVER MENDARO

Complete and Unabridged

LINFORD
Leicester

First hardcover edition published in Great Britain
in 2002 by Robert Hale Limited, London
Originally published in paperback as
'Lone Gun Renegade' by Tex Kirby

First Linford Edition
published 2004
by arrangement with
Robert Hale Limited, London

The moral right of the author has been asserted

All the characters in this book are fictional, and
any resemblance to persons, living or dead,
is purely coincidental.

Copyright © 1971, 2002 by John Glasby
All rights reserved

British Library CIP Data

Adams, James, 1928 –
    Storm over Mendaro.—Large print ed.—
Linford western library
    1. Western stories 2. Large type books
    I. Title II. Kirby, Tex. Lone gun renegade
    823.9'14 [F]

ISBN 1–84395–258–0

Published by
F. A. Thorpe (Publishing)
Anstey, Leicestershire

Set by Words & Graphics Ltd.
Anstey, Leicestershire
Printed and bound in Great Britain by
T. J. International Ltd., Padstow, Cornwall
This book is printed on acid-free paper

1

Rough Justice

The rain had started shortly before dawn and now it was a steady, beating downpour that seeped from the overcast heavens, dripping from the wide brim of Brad Lando's hat, running in rivulets down his face. At times, it thickened into a mist, shutting out his view of the surrounding terrain so that it was impossible to see more than fifty yards in any direction. Underfoot, the ground was a slippery sea of mud in which Big Jet slid for hours.

He had ridden close on a hundred miles in the past week along this border trail seeing no one. The main trails all ran far to the north where the wagon trains were heading west, filled with men seeking their fortune and a new life among the rich valleys of California.

There had been times when he wished that he had ridden the same way, hitching up with some train and putting as much distance between himself and this god-forsaken land as possible; but too many things had happened along the way and it was impossible for a man to turn back the clock and ride the same trail twice.

Big Jet slid suddenly, scrambling in a desperate effort to keep his feet on ground that was as slick as axle grease. They careened down a short slope, finishing up among the rocks at the bottom. As the black stallion went down on its haunches, Brad threw himself from the saddle, hit the rocks hard and lay still for several moments as pain jarred through his leg. Then, with an effort, he pushed himself to his feet. Muddy water coursed swiftly along the rocks, swirling icily around his ankles. Staring about him through the wreathing mist, he tried to make out details of his surroundings. Only the gods knew where he could find shelter in this desolate country.

Somewhere ahead of him lay Mendaro. From what he knew of the place, it was a barren frontier town, hewn out of the uncompromising desert to form a gateway into the south and west. Less than ten miles from the border with Mexico, herders used it to drive their cattle through, taking them at times up to the railroad and at others as far south as the Rio Grande. There were others who used it too as a crossing point into Mexico, running guns and ammunition to renegades on both sides of the border.

As he caught at the reins, leading his mount into the slanting rain, he thought again of the message which had reached him in Tucson; a telegraph message from Jeb Callaghan offering him a job if he would ride out as far as Mendaro. He knew little of Callaghan apart from what his father had told him; how they had headed west together more than thirty years before with Callaghan finally riding south towards Mexico, starting up as a rancher close to the border.

What the job was, he didn't know, but with only five dollars to rub together and a strong desire to put Senorro and Shiloh and all the other places where he had met with only violence and gunplay behind him, anything was worth considering. He mounted up as they came out on to a broad plateau. Here the ground was more rocky, all of the water having flowed off the sides, cascading down into the mist.

About a mile further on, the mist thinned a little and he spotted something by the side of the trail. Gigging his mount towards it, he felt the sudden tightening of his stomach muscles as he made out what it was. The two corpses swung listlessly from the stout limb of the tree which overhung the trail. In spite of his training, Big Jet shied away nervously and Brad was forced to keep a tight-fisted grip on the reins to hold him steady.

'Easy there, boy,' he murmured softly. Sitting forward in the saddle, he surveyed the grim scene for several moments, then touched spurs to the stallion's flanks and moved on past. There had been nothing to indicate who those two men were, nor the nature of their crime. Both, however, had been fancily dressed and he judged that neither was the ordinary run of outlaw. More than ever it reminded him sharply that he had entered the country of the trail-blazers, the gamblers and cut-throats, crossing the frontier that divided the more law-abiding territory from that of the lawless breed.

Pushing on through the hills, he came down into a wide, scrub-dotted plain. After a while, the rain eased off and the sun broke through the thinning clouds. Around him, as the heat increased, the terrain steamed, giving up its moisture to the heavens. By mid-afternoon, the sun was beating down on him like the heat rays from hell and the dust from the rocks came up from beneath his mount's hoofs in tiny brown puffs, hanging dryly in the still air so that his nose and throat were burning with it. Even the mesquite was covered with a thin film of it so that it had a queer, dead-looking appearance.

The only splashes of colour he saw, apart from the eternal redness of the sandstone, were the darting lizards and the occasional coiled length of a rattler. He rested Big Jet for an hour beside a muddy waterhole, then moved on through scattered pine stands and over rocky ground, entering a narrow draw overgrown with brush. As he moved through it, he felt the gentle rise and when it finally opened he was high up on a wide bench that looked down on a broad valley with a sluggish river running through it and the tops of the pines far below. It was there that he made out the grey pall of smoke that drifted slowly across the plain from a point close to the river.

Further on, some three or four miles distant, a diminishing cloud of dust caught and held his attention for several moments. Emotion stirred in him, tinged with apprehension. Spurring Big Jet down the tricky slope, he headed out across the plain, shortening the distance between himself and the burning buildings. Smoke eddied back to him as he approached, stinging the back of his throat.

Dropping from the saddle on the run, he stared about him for any sign of life. Those riders who had hit this place had made a thorough job of it. Close by, the barn was an inferno with the sharp crackle of the flames as they ate through the store of hay roaring in his ears. The ranch house itself was well alight, with flames licking up the stout timber posts and already the roof was burning in several places. There was no answering response to his yell and he went forward cautiously, holding his kerchief around his nose and mouth, fighting his way through the thick, enveloping smoke. Eyes watering, he tried to see his way inside, fumbling over a smouldering beam that had crashed down, half-blocking the doorway.

Tugging frantically at the wood, he hauled it clear, plunged into the room that lay beyond. Tears streaming from his eyes, blurring his vision, made it difficult to see clearly. Halfway across the debris-littered floor, he stumbled over something soft and yielding. Going down on one knee, he turned the body over, felt a wave of sickness grip him, churning his muscles. The woman could not have been much more than twenty-five years old. There was an ugly red stain on her dress, just over her heart. Evidently she had died quickly. The rifle lying beside her told of a futile attempt to protect herself against the murdering band who had done this. Stunned, he got to his feet, forced his way through into the room at the back. This was clearly the kitchen. There was a pile of dishes stacked neatly by the sink and an iron pot on the stove.

The flames were now beginning to

eat their way into this part of the house, but here the smoke was not quite as thick and brushing the tears from his eyes with the back of his hand, he stared about him. For a moment he figured the room was empty. Then a low moan from the corner reached him and in the gloom he made out the figure of a man lying on his side against the wall just beneath the window.

Swiftly, Brad went over, eased the other into a more comfortable position. There was blood on the man's face, trickling down from a deep gash across his forehead where a slug had sliced obliquely across the skull.

For a second, the other tried to feebly fight him off, but lacked the strength to do more than push him away slightly.

'Take it easy now,' Brad said quietly.

'Who are you, mister? One o' that murderin' gang?'

Brad shook his head. 'I spotted 'em ridin' off while I was up on the plateau. Weren't no chance of catchin' up with 'em, so I came here to see if I could help.'

'Nothin' you can do now,' grunted the other. A spasm of pain twisted his features into a grimace. He turned his head, glancing about him, an anxious look in his eyes.

'Better let me get you out of here.' Brad laid a hand on the other's arm. 'This fire is spreadin' mighty quick. That roof is goin' to come down any minute.'

'Where's — ?'

After a long moment, Brad said softly: 'She's dead, friend. They must've shot her before they fired the place.' Gently, he lifted the other to his feet, tightening his grip as the man swayed against the wall. 'Think you can stand?'

With a supreme effort, the other drew himself upright, pulling a harsh breath down into his lungs. His eyes had grown bleak and there was a sudden hard set to his face. For a moment, he seemed on the point of breaking up completely then he pulled himself together, lips compressed into a hard, straight line.

'Where's Ellie?'

'Back there in the parlour. But there's nothin' — '

The other made for the door, throwing off Brad's restraining hand. Before he could reach it there came a grinding crash from almost directly overhead. Lunging forward, Brad caught the other about the middle, pulled him back sharply. Splintered beams, flames running in licking, red tongues along their length, smashed down into the opening, blocking it utterly.

Savagely, Brad hauled the man back. Swinging with a sudden cry, the other struggled against him, bringing up his fist. Ducking the blow, Brad recognised the look of grief and hysteria on the other's face. Before the man could recover from his wild swing, he hammered a short blow to the exposed chin, felt the other sag against him, his eyes glazing over. Bending, he took the man's inert weight across his shoulders, turned and moved towards the back door, kicking it down with his foot. Once outside, he carried his burden well away from the blazing ranch house, then laid him on the ground, gasping air down gratefully into his heaving lungs.

Slowly, his vision cleared and the pounding in his chest eased. Behind him, the roof gave with a cavernous roar, sending a shower of sparks high into the air, a final streak of flame lifting with them, tapering off into the pall of smoke.

Whistling up Big Jet, he pulled his canteen from the saddlehorn, splashed some of the water into the unconscious man's face. The other stirred, twisted his head sharply, eyes flicking open. Wiping his face, he forced himself into a sitting position.

'You feel like talkin' now?' Brad asked.

The other hesitated, then nodded numbly. Shock was still deep within him, clouding his mind.

'Those men who did this? You know who they were?'

'Sure, sure.' The words came out mechanically. 'Mendoza and his bunch. Who else?'

Squatting back on his haunches, Brad let his glance roam over the burning buildings. 'You must've some idea why they did this to you?'

The man's bleak eyes settled on him for a long moment. Then the withdrawn look faded and one of intense anger replaced it, curling his lips into a vicious snarl. 'You must be a stranger around these parts, Mister — to ask a damn stupid question like that.'

Brad was puzzled by the other's attitude, but tried again. 'All right, so I just rode in.'

The other nodded dumbly. 'There were maybe a dozen outfits here in the valley a couple of years ago. Spite of all the trouble around Mendaro, the place was peaceful enough. Then the rustlin' and the shootin' started. Some of the outfits went under when the bank refused to extend their loan, said it was too big a risk with all the trouble we was havin'. That was when Jess Forlan came around. He offered us all protection against Mendoza and his gang if we agreed to pay him a couple of thousand dollars a year.'

'And you agreed?'

'It was either that or lose everything we'd fought for,' muttered the other listlessly. He seemed now to have sunk into an attitude of apathy. 'For the first six months everythin' was like it was before. Then Forlan put up his price, more'n doubled it. Nobody could afford to pay. We tried to organize ourselves to fight, but it was useless. We ain't seasoned gunslingers.'

So that was the way of it. Brad nodded his head slowly. It sounded like the old story of land grabbers, men filled with greed and the desire to dominate the entire territory.

'Did it ever occur to you that Forlan might be workin' with these half-breeds? Seems to me that he's doin' just that. Funny they should stop attackin' you just so long as you pay him his blood money.'

'We figured there might be somethin' in that, but there was no proof and as far as the law in Mendaro is concerned, it's a case of the man who has the most guns to back his play comin' out on top.'

As it was explained, the situation here was grim in its simplicity.

'How far is it into Mendaro?' Brad asked.

'Ten miles or so. Due south.'

Brad got to his feet, stood looking down at the other, then swung his glance to take in the scene of carnage all about him. 'Guess there's no reason for you to stick around here. You feel up to ridin' into town?'

The other's lips went slack. 'What's in Mendaro for me?' he said thinly.

'Could be that we'll meet up with some of the hombres who did this. You ain't goin' to take it lyin' down, are you?'

He noticed the spark at the back of the man's eyes as he struggled to his feet. Some of the steel and fire came back into him. It would be a long time before he forgot this, forgot the woman who lay dead inside that pile of smouldering wreckage, but at least he now had something to fasten on to, something to set his sights on.

'Let's go,' he said hoarsely. He hobbled away from the burning shell of the ranch house, swinging around the side. Brad followed, leading Big Jet. How long the other would go on without breaking down, he didn't know. At the moment, all he could do was push the man to the limit, otherwise it could be the finish of the other.

As they approached the barn, a bay came trotting into view from the brush. There was a saddle hanging over one of the posts and the rancher threw it over the animal, tightened the cinch, then swung slowly into the saddle, his face bleak, staring straight ahead of him but seeing nothing.

Brad mounted up and drew alongside. 'My name's Lando,' he said quietly

'Lawson — Dave Lawson,' muttered the other dully. He thrust his Winchester into the scabbard mechanically.

★   ★   ★

The heat of late afternoon was a hot blanket over them. Dust lifted from beneath their mounts and swallowed them in an orange-yellow cloud. Brad continually checked their back-trail, still feeling a mite uneasy in his mind, but the rolling range was empty and three miles beyond the river, even the last vestiges of smoke were gone from the flat horizon.

Darkness fell swiftly, but two hours later they spotted lights ahead of them and, kicking their horses into a run, they hit the main street of Mendaro half an hour later.

Brad rode his mount on a short rein, searching for the lawman's office, found it crushed between the bank and the stage depot. There was a light showing through the window facing the street. Swinging down, he hitched the reins to the rail and walked up on to the boardwalk with Lawson close on his heels.

There was no answer to his first knock and he rapped again, louder this time and more insistently.

'All right. Hold on, damn you!'

The voice was gruff and sullen, that of an impatient man. A few seconds later, the door was wrenched open and a big, broad-shouldered man stood framed in the opening. He eyed Brad up and down appraisingly, then flicked his glance towards the rancher. In the shadowed face, Brad could make out little detail beyond a thick, black moustache and brooding, suspicious eyes.

'Well? What the hell is it?'

'We're here to report a killin' and the burnin' down of a ranch,' Brad said thinly. 'You think we can do it inside?'

The lawman's jaw dropped open slackly in surprise, then he stepped back, an expression of hostility on his broad, fleshy features. As the two men entered, he shifted across towards the desk, assuming an authoritative stance, studying them coolly, his right hand hovering close to his gunbutt.

'You're Dave Lawson, ain't you?' he demanded, glaring at Brad's companion.

'That's right. It was my place those killers burned down. They killed Ellie. Shot her down in cold blood, then fired the place.'

'I'm mighty sorry to hear that, Lawson.' The other sat down, made no offer of a chair to either of them. Brad hesitated for a moment, feeling anger rise inside him. Then he walked over, hooked his leg around the chair in front of the desk and motioned Lawson to sit down. He deliberately ignored the look which the sheriff threw in his direction. There had been nothing in the other's tone to indicate that he really meant what he had said.

'You know the identity of these men?' The lawman shifted his weight in his chair.

'Of course I do. It was Mendoza and his gang of gunhawks.'

'Accordin' to what I've heard, these men always ride masked. How can you be certain it was them?'

'You think I can't recognise those murderin' half-breeds when I see 'em?' There was a rising inflection in the other's tone. 'They killed Ellie and I'm sure as hell goin' to see that they hang for it.'

'Now hold on there.' A sudden change came over the sheriff. 'You can't go around makin' statements like that in Mendaro without any proof. In the first place, there are more'n half a dozen gangs operating this side of the border, ridin' over and then pullin' back before we can do anythin' to stop 'em.'

'You ever tried to do anythin'?' There was an insolence in Brad's tone that stung the other. He swung sharply to face him, an uplift of anger seizing him.

'You shoot your mouth off like that any more, Mister, and I'll lock you up inside the jail for contempt of the law.'

'You can try, Sheriff.' He locked his gaze hard with the other's until the lawman looked away. 'But it seems to me that there's somethin' almighty strange goin' on here when killers can ride in and burn down a man's home and get clean away with it without the law tryin' to do anythin' about it. You figure maybe that it's Lawson's fault this happened? The way you're talkin', sure seems that way to me.'

'Maybe it is,' snapped the other harshly. 'He knew what the territory was like when he came here. This is frontier country. The big law ain't reached here yet and if we try to go up against that gang, we wouldn't stand a chance.'

'Seems like this hombre Forlan did all right so long as he got paid blood money to do it.'

'What Jess Forlan does is his own business and I'd advise you to remember that if you intend stickin' around in Mendaro.' The other thrust himself heavily to his feet; dull spots of colour suffusing his cheeks. 'He's a mighty big man around town as you'll find out if you start shootin' your mouth off outside this office. Just who are you, Mister, and what's your particular beef about this incident?'

'Brad Lando. I guess you can say that I don't like to see men burned out of their homes and their kin killed by killers and thieves.'

The other ran his tongue around his lips and uttered a low curse. 'I've seen hombres like you before, Lando. Dogooders who try to set the world to rights. The cemetery yonder is full of 'em. Be careful you don't go the same way.'

'To hell with you, Sheriff. We came here lookin' for help from the law.' He stared around at Lawson. 'Guess we ain't goin' to get it. Reckon we might as well leave right now and not take up any more of the sheriff's precious time.'

He made for the door as he spoke, heard Lawson scrape back his chair and get to his feet.

Then the sheriff said harshly: 'Hold it right there, Lawson.' He had risen to his feet and there was a levelled Colt in his right fist, the barrel trained on Brad's chest.

'I don't take that kind of talk from anybody, least of all a whipper-snapper who rides into town and starts talkin' like he owns the goddam place.' There was a wolfish look on his face now and Brad knew that the other was not far removed from pulling that trigger. He moved forward purposefully until he stood a few feet from Brad. 'I'd as soon kill you as spit, Lando.'

'You ain't goin' to kill anybody, Kerdy,' interposed Lawson harshly. 'This man saved my life and I'll yell so goddam loud if you so much as make a move to pull that trigger that the stink will go clear to the Mexican border and beyond.'

'Don't you bet on that, Lawson. I can kill you too — and get away with it.'

The sheriff swung his gaze slightly as Lawson moved around to his right. His attention was distracted for less than two seconds, but for Brad, it was more than enough. His hand slashed down at the other's wrist, slamming it hard just above the joint. Before the gun hit the floor, he had hauled the other around, bringing his arm up high against his shoulder blades. Kerdy uttered an explosive gasp, face contorted.

'I ain't got much time for lawmen like you, Kerdy,' Brad said evenly through his teeth. 'I figure a little while in one of your own cells might suffice to cool you off a little.'

He nodded towards the rancher, saw the other hesitate for a moment, then move towards the wall, plucking the bunch of keys off the hook. With a savage movement, he thrust the lawman ahead of him, down the short passage and into one of the bare cells at the back. Slamming the door, he twisted the key sharply in the lock before stepping back into the middle of the passage.

Gripping the bars tightly with his fists, Kerdy thrust his face close up against them, eyes bright like a rattler's. 'You'll regret this, Lando — and you too, Lawson. I'll have this whole town up and after you before nightfall. There ain't no place where you can hide. And by hell, when I find you, I'll see you hang.'

Brad stared the other out for several moments, then turned on his heel and walked back into the front office, putting the keys back on to the hook. Lawson looked up from his position near the door. Worry was written all over his face.

'We'd better get the hell out of here, Lando. That was a damn fool thing we did, locking Kerdy up in his own jail.'

Reflecting on it, Brad knew that the other was right. But what had been done in the heat of the moment, could not be easily undone and there was not the slightest doubt in his mind that the sheriff would have shot them both down without compunction.

Reaching the boardwalk, he threw a swift glance up and down the street, then hustled the other towards the waiting horses. As they mounted up, he said harshly: 'You ever heard of a man named Callaghan?'

'Jeb Callaghan?'

'That's right. He's a friend of mine. We can trust him. He'll let us hole up for a while until we can figure out what to do next.'

'He runs the Flying Y spread down by Clearwater Spring. You sure he's a friend of yours?'

'Sure. Why? Somethin' on your mind?' There had been an odd edge to the other's tone which Brad noticed instantly.

'Not really. Just that he's got the reputation of bein' a queer sort of cuss. There's a heap of talk about him too. Seems he's about the only rancher so far who's not been troubled by

Mendoza. Reckon you can imagine the way the talk goes.'

'I can guess.' Brad nodded grimly. 'No reason to judge a man before you know all the facts though. Let's ride before Kerdy rouses the whole place.' They could just hear the yells of the outraged lawman echoing from inside the building.

Hauling on the reins, he moved towards the middle of the street. It was completely dark now, cooler than it had been since the storm and over to the south-east, a round yellow moon climbed majestically into the heavens. They rode slowly so as not to attract any unwelcome attention. Mendaro gave Brad the impression of a town just waiting to erupt; an uneasy sort of place, too full of shadows for his liking.

Working their way past the two saloons which stood side by side halfway along the main street, Brad eyed the bunch of horses tethered outside. His keen-eyed gaze took in the trappings, telling him at once that they belonged to no ordinary cowpokes. These horses had come from south of the Mexico border and the man who lounged somnolently against the batwing doors of the nearer saloon was swarthy-faced with the unmistakable look of a half-breed about him.

As they drew level with the other, Brad saw the man suddenly push himself away from the wooden upright, saw a faint gust of expression flash over the leering features. Then the man had whirled abruptly, diving back through the doors. Edging his mount over to Lawson's, he said harshly: 'I smell trouble. Better keep your eyes open. That hombre yonder must've recognized you as we rode by.'

The other turned his head sharply, seemed to notice the horses for the first time. His eyes narrowed down and he reached sideways for the Winchester. Brad caught at his arm, shook his head.

'No! There must be close on a score of them in there. We don't stand a

28

chance, even if they are the killers who hit your place.'

Indecision was strong on the other's face and for a moment he seemed on the point of arguing the matter. Then he straightened in the saddle, touched spurs to the bay's flanks, heading along the deserted street after Brad. A sudden shout lifted behind them as they rode and, throwing a swift glance over his shoulder, Brad caught a fragmentary glimpse of the crowd of men who came pushing out on to the boardwalk staring after them.

They rode headlong out of town into the growing moonlight, cut up into the barren ground which pushed its shoulders hard down against the trail. Taking in a deep breath, Brad felt the cold rush of air against his face. The lights of Mendaro faded into the distance behind them as they gave their mounts their heads.

They covered the best part of a mile before Lawson slowed and twisted in the saddle, studying the landmarks.

'You figure they're followin' us, Lando?' he asked through his teeth.

'You'd better bet on it,' Brad muttered grimly. 'Any way we can get off this trail?'

'Another half mile and we reach a ford,' Lawson told him. 'There's a track there on the other side of the river, leads down through an arroyo. Plenty of cover on either side and there's a spot just east of the track where the growth is pretty heavy. We could make a stand there if we have to but there's also a good chance they'll ride by without spottin' us.'

Five minutes later, they pushed their horses across the shallow ford, swung down a long slope and across the arroyo, slashed with midnight shadows thrown by the moon. Ahead of him, Lawson drew rein, slipped from the saddle, dragging his mount after him through the thick, impeding growth.

'This should do it,' Brad said thinly. He looked about him. The river was just visible in the distance, shimmering yellowly in the reflected moonlight. The rocks of the arroyo were just visible where they cut up against the starlit heavens. 'Now we'll just take it easy and await developments. From here we can see and hear them comin' long before they'll be able to sight us. If they cut across the river and keep on goin', all so well and good. If they don't — ' He fingered his Colt meaningly, checked the chambers.

He was not quite as confident as his companion seemed to be, for he was experiencing an uneasy presentiment that those men trailing them were not likely to be thrown off their trail by such a simple ruse as this. Why he should feel it so strongly, he hadn't the slightest idea, but he did.

2

Flying Y

The wait was not a long one. The riders must have lit out of Mendaro immediately after they had pulled out. In the moonlight, Brad spotted them some time before the sound of their mounts reached him. There were half a dozen of them, crowding together along the trail and as they reached the water's edge, they slowed their mounts, bending forward in the saddle. Brad had heard how well these half-breeds could track a man, even in moonlight and over rocks where there was scarcely a print to be seen.

One of the men suddenly pointed up towards the arroyo, said something in a harsh tone. Lawson drew the rifle from its scabbard, cocked it, then shook his head. The distance was still too great for him to get in a killing shot and there was no sense in giving away their position until they had to.

Now the riders had splashed through the water, were climbing up on to the bank. Lawson estimated the distance again, went down on his knees behind one of the rocks, resting the barrel of the Winchester across it, sighting along it. His lips were drawn back into a vicious grin, teeth showing whitely in his shadowed face.

The riders had begun to swing their mounts down toward the arroyo. Brad waited until they rode into the far end, then scuttled off to his right, dropping down behind the protecting boulders. The half-breeds were urging their reluctant mounts through the tough, wiry scrub, cursing loudly as they came on. Out of the corner of his eye, he saw Lawson clamp the butt of the rifle hard in against his shoulder, his body hunched forward, just visible in the flooding moonlight.

The hammering blast of the Winchester rang out like thunder among the rocks. Squinting into the moonlight, Brad saw one of the oncoming men suddenly throw up his arms and topple sideways out of the saddle as if he had been kicked in the chest by a mule. The Winchester belched smoke and flame a second time but scored a miss. Then there came answering flashes as the band dispersed, swinging their mounts towards the looming walls of the arroyo. They had been caught in the open, taken by surprise.

But they were not long in recovering themselves. Recognizing that they still held the superiority in numbers, the men began drifting forward, still hugging the shadows, but no longer quite as cautious as before. So far, Brad had held his fire, leaving it up to Lawson to use the greater power of his weapon. Now he saw that this had paid off. To his left, a small group of men suddenly darted forward from cover and began edging towards Lawson's hideout. Evidently they figured that both of them were holed up there, for he saw that within a few moments they would be less than twenty feet from where he crouched.

Pulling his lips back over his teeth, he waited tensely. There was the dull flash of moonlight glinting off drawn weapons and pale blurs that were faces beneath the wide-brimmed hats. Lawson sent a couple of shots whining along the length of the arroyo. Then the three men in front of Brad exploded into action. One of them uttered a loud yell as he ran, feet slipping on the treacherous ground. Brad let them come alongside his vantage point, then sent a ripple of shots crashing into them from the side.

The nearest man went over backward, cursing shrilly, clutching at a smashed shoulder. The other two slithered to a halt, whirled, loosing off a couple of shots in Brad's direction, firing blindly with the moonlight in their eyes. A slug ricocheted over his head, whining into the distance. More firing came from the opposite side of the arroyo, a vicious crossfire that forced him to keep his head down.

Flinging all caution to the wind, the two half-breeds lurched in his direction, firing as they came. Bullets stormed above Brad's prone form. One stung his cheek with a red-hot touch, throwing him momentarily off balance. Then he recovered himself, shot right and left. One of the men plunged forward on to his face, lay still, his body sprawled out over the rocks. The other blundered forward and as Brad pulled the trigger, aiming up at the other's tall figure, the man discharged a single shot, unable to miss at that distance.

The jagged flame from the other's Colt seared across Brad's vision, seemed to fill the whole of creation. The thunder of it roared in his ears in the split second before the sky darkened and fell on him.

★   ★   ★

When Brad Lando recovered consciousness, he realized that someone was bending over him, a dark shape outlined against the heavens. Shivering, his head a dull suffusing ache, he lay for a moment staring up at the other with unseeing eyes. Then, gradually, the fog lifted from his mind, he recognized Dave Lawson and forced himself into a sitting position. Agony lanced and stabbed at him and his stomach muscles churned with nausea. With an effort, he forced it away, shaking his head to clear it.

'Here, let me give you a hand.' Lawson caught him by the arms and urged him to his feet.

Swaying, Brad leaned against the other for a moment, sucking air down into his lungs, blinking his eyes rapidly. Twisting his head, he stared about him, peering into the long, moonthrown shadows.

'Nothin' to fear from those coyotes for the time bein',' Lawson said thinly. 'After you cut down those three yonder, the rest backed off across the river.'

Brad lifted trembling fingers to his forehead, felt the crustiness of blood on the lacerated flesh where the slug had sliced across his temple just above the left eye. It had been touch-and-go. Half an inch to the right and it would have been the finish of him.

'How many of those critters are still out there?' he asked thinly.

'Can't be more than two or three. They were in such a goddamn hurry to get out that I only caught a brief glimpse of 'em. Then I saw that you'd been hit. You feelin' all right, Lando?'

'I've felt better, but I doubt if it'll worry me any.' He glanced across to where their horses stood waiting. 'You see anythin' of those half-breeds?'

Lawson crawled away with his head well down. Brad heard the scrape of his boots as he edged up among the rocks. When he came back, he pointed off towards the far bank of the river. 'I just spotted 'em yonder. They're sittin' their mounts, waiting. Wonder what they've got in mind for us.'

'They know damn well they can't prise us out of here so long as we stick among these rocks. We can watch every trail up here and drop 'em before they can spot us. They've got all the time in the world. They know they've only got to wait until mornin' and then the boot will be on the other foot. And if we try to ride out before dawn, they'll be ready to cut out after us, and in the open, they'll have the advantage.'

'So what do we do?'

'Well, you know this place better than I do. We either get out of here without bein' seen or heard, or we go down and take on those three hombres. Which is it to be?'

'Ain't no point tryin' to finish them hombres,' grunted the other tightly. 'I'm almost plumb out of shells.'

'That settles it then. We've got to get out of here right now, before they pluck up enough courage to come in after us.'

Everything was quiet as they moved stealthily into the looming rocks with

Lawson leading the way, yet all the time Brad was conscious of life and movement all about him, creeping, moving things all around them. As he slid through narrow gaps in the boulders, trailing Big Jet behind him on a tight rein, he wondered why those three men had not ensured against them escaping like this by sending a man up to watch the far side of these rocky upthrusts, where they opened out into the flatland once more. Not until they climbed higher among the rocky ledges, following the only trail there was, did he discover the reason. Here that trail which wound along that smooth rock wall was less than a couple of feet wide at the most and off to his left there was a sheer drop of a hundred feet or more, down on to needle-sharp rocks which yawned hungrily below, waiting to split him if he fell.

In places, the trail angled sharply around outthrusting faces of rock and he was forced to shuffle forward an inch at a time, pressing his back and shoulders hard against the sandstone, not daring to look down. How the animals made it, he never knew. Then, to his relief, the track widened, it became possible for them to walk beside their mounts as they cut down through deep gorges which slashed the plateau.

At the bottom of the long slope, the ground ran on unbroken for perhaps half a mile and then they came to the boundary fence which had been strung across the trail. Slowly, they worked their way along it until they came to the wide gate, flanked by two white pillars of stone.

'It sure looks as though he made out well for himself,' Brad remarked, taking in everything.

'Like I said, for some reason he ain't been troubled none by the same things as the rest of us.' There was a trace of bitterness in Lawson's tone. 'Maybe if he'd had that to face up to — '

Brad jerked up a hand, cutting the other off in mid-sentence. A couple of

41

riders topped a low rise off to their right, paced their mounts in their direction. One trailed a shotgun across his saddlehorn.

After a long moment, a harsh voice came sharply.

'Who are you men?'

Keeping his hands well in sight, Brad called back: 'The name's Brad Lando. I got a wire from Jeb Callaghan when I was in Tucson askin' me to ride out this way.'

There was a moment's conversation between the two men, then the man with the shotgun came on, his eyes sharp. 'Who's this other hombre?'

'Dave Lawson. Mendoza's gang hit his ranch today. He's all right, I can vouch for him.'

'Until we're sure you're who you say you are, you'll vouch for nobody, friend.' The other gestured with his weapon. 'Ride on in and keep your hands where we can see 'em. We'll ride on to the line camp. You can go on to the ranch tomorrow.'

'Suits me.' Brad gigged Big Jet forward through the gate with Lawson trailing him. More and more, it came to him how uneasy this neck of the territory was, where no man's word could be trusted. There was the suspicion in him now that Callaghan had sent for him, not simply as a friend, but in order to get another gun.

Five minutes later, a couple of small adobe buildings loomed up in the moonlight with a pin-point of light piercing the gloom. A door opened as they approached and two men came out.

'That you, Flint?' called one uncertainly.

'It's me,' replied the other. 'We picked up a couple of hombres at the east gate. One of 'em claims to be Brad Lando.' He swung down from the saddle, motioned Brad and Lawson to do likewise. So far, these men had not taken their guns and Brad felt sure that they were half-convinced, that Callaghan must have had them on the look out for him.

Then he was through the door and inside the nearer hut, blinking a little in the light of the two storm lanterns swinging from one of the overhead beams. Another three men were inside, seated around a long table, a couple of whisky bottles in front of them and a pack of grubby cards in front of one of them.

The dealer stared hard at them for a moment, then said tightly: 'You're Lawson, ain't you? You got a spread along the river apiece.'

'I had a spread there,' said the other bitterly. 'It ain't there any more.'

'Mendoza?'

'That's right. They rode in just before noon. Killed Ellie and then fired the place. That was when Lando rode by.'

The other nodded, got to his feet. 'Better let Hal take a look at that head wound. You look like you got quite a bump there, Mister.' He turned his glance on Brad.

'I've been hit harder before,' Brad said nonchalantly. He seated himself in one of the chairs, aware for the first time that day of the deep weariness in him. There were six bunks over by two of the walls and he reckoned that this was more than just a line camp. Generally, the cowhands built themselves a fire wherever they happened to spend the night and wrapped themselves in their bedrolls. These men, too, were not ordinary range riders. The number of guns and rifles testified to that. Clearly they were here on more warlike business than just tending to cattle. More than likely there was a full-scale range war in the offing and Callaghan was taking no unnecessary chances on being jumped. Maybe, he reflected, this was why he had not been hit like the other ranchers in the area. He seemed to have plenty of men to protect the spread, men who knew how to handle themselves in a gunfight.

The big man named Flint poured out some coffee and then ladled a couple of plates of beans from the kettle over the stove. He no longer seemed quite as suspicious or hostile as when they had first met.

When he had eaten his fill, he leaned back in his chair and rolled himself a cigarette, aware of the glances laid on him. Drawing the smoke into his lungs, he said quietly: 'Callaghan didn't say why he wanted me out here though judgin' from what's happened since I rode into this territory, I'd say that he was more than keen to hire a fast gun than a man handy with a rope and a brandin' iron.'

One of the men laughed harshly, shut up as the big man laid a hard glance on him. Hitching his chair closer to Brad, he leaned his weight on his elbows.

'You're pretty shrewd, Lando. You'll hear all of it from the boss tomorrow, I reckon. But you're right when you say there's trouble brewin' around here. Somebody is tryin' to drive the ranchers out of this territory. They're usin' every low-down trick in the book to do it. Most of the smaller spreads have already gone to the wall. If we

46

didn't patrol the Flying Y every single night, the same would happen here. We've lost four good men in the past month, shot down from ambush. More than five hundred head of good beef have gone a-missin' and you can take it from me that things are goin' to get a sight worse before they get any better.'

'What about this fella Forlan I've been hearin' about? Think he could be at the back of it all?'

'Jess Forlan? He's in this for all he can get out of it for sure. But he's nothin' more than a big blowhard. He runs the bank in Mendaro. True, he called in the mortgages of some of the smaller ranchers and he offered to protect 'em against Mendoza — for a price.'

'And so long as they paid that price, it seems to have worked,' put in Lawson. 'So he's got some pull with that Mex bandit.'

'If you want to keep a whole hide on you around town, I'd keep your lip buttoned up as far as Forlan is concerned. He's a pretty big man and he didn't get where he is now without trampin' on anybody who gets in his way.'

'If I find that he was at the back of those killers who shot Ellie, then he'll have to answer to me,' declared the rancher savagely. 'I got nothin' to lose now.'

One of the card players at the table leaned back suddenly, and said: 'I'm turnin' in now. What about the rest of you?'

Flint gave a brief nod. 'I'll take the watch until three with Morgan. The rest of you get some sleep.' He looked towards Brad. 'There are a couple of spare bunks yonder you can have for the night. I'll get one of the boys to ride with you to the ranch at sunup.'

*   *   *

Jeb Callaghan was a tall, slender man in his late fifties, his hair greying at the temples, his face creased into a permanent frown of worry. He greeted Brad and Lawson civilly and ushered them into the parlour, nodding towards a couple of chairs before seating himself. Pouring a couple of drinks, he lit a black cheroot, blew the smoke towards the ceiling, staring at them unwinkingly even though the smoke laced across his eyes.

'I'm glad you managed to make it, Brad,' he said quietly. 'I rode with your father years ago and if you're anythin' like him then you're the kind of man I need around here.'

Brad grinned. 'From what I saw last night at the line camp, I'd say you've got yourself plenty of men handy with a gun.'

'Sure, sure. But it's gettin' more and more difficult to keep good men. Every week, one or more of 'em forks his bronc and rides on over the hill. Can't say I blame 'em. Things have been rough these past few months. I pay gunhawk's wages, but that don't mean a thing to a man if he don't live long enough to spend it.'

'As bad as that?'

'Worse. This whole territory is goin' to blow wide apart at the seams any time. What with those human wolves who strike across the border without any warnin' and those other two-legged coyotes in Mendaro, just waitin' to grab the best pickings once we're all finished.'

'I can see your problem,' Brad conceded.

'Then you'll take the job? It won't be easy and I won't hide the fact that there's danger. You've run into some of it already, I gather.'

Brad nodded. 'Some,' he admitted. 'I came here hopin' to find a place where I could forget about trouble. Seems I was dead wrong.'

'You were. Time will tell just how wrong.' Callaghan's tone was deadly serious. He let go a tight, meagre smile.

'How far can you trust the men you've got?'

The other shrugged, pursed his lips

into a hard line. 'Those who've been with me for some time, I can vouch for. The others I've had to hire to fight this menace, I can't. They're gunslingers. I take what I can get. Why? You figure some of 'em might be workin' for somebody else? Feeding information back to those Mexes?'

'It's happened before. They want to know where your cattle are, how many men are watchin' the herd. Then they move in at the right time and rustle 'em off without any danger to themselves.'

Callaghan's face assumed a taut, speculative look. He stared down at the glowing cheroot, turning it over and over in his fingers. 'If that's so, then I need a man I can trust more than ever. I'll pay you top wages so long as you work for me.'

'That sounds fair enough. I assume the same goes for Lawson here?'

'All right.'

'And one other thing. I play this my way. That might mean you'll come up against the law in Mendaro. I've already had a brush with that sheriff there.'

Callaghan made an impatient gesture. 'I've got no time for men like Kerdy. He's no real lawman. Just a jumped-up gunhawk put into office by the mayor and a few other citizens. For reasons best known to himself, Mayor Eversham has been swearing in as deputies the worst sort of killer this side of the Mexico border. Between them they manage to keep Mendaro in a state of complete subjection. I'll back you against Kerdy and any of his men.'

'That's good enough for us.' Brad got to his feet. 'I'll take the job.'

Relief showed on the other's face. 'I was hopin' you'd say that. We'll drink to it.' He filled the glasses, downed his own in a single gulp, a dull flush coming to his face. Brad tossed the whisky down, eyeing the other closely as he did so. He had the feeling that Callaghan was a man close to cracking up; a man who had been under a tremendous strain, both physical and mental, for a long time and had almost reached his breaking point.

*   *   *

Cutting out of the wide courtyard the following morning, Brad eased Big Jet into a slow trot. Northward as far as he could see were the rolling grasslands, stretching towards the blue-hazed mountains which stood majestically along the wide skyline, the rugged foothills, cold and desolate, standing beneath them. The ranches lay in that direction, those which were still in existence and the others which had been taken over by the bank in Mendaro. Brad's lips thinned down a little as he digested that thought. The Mendaro bank was merely a front to hide Jess Forlan; of that he was certain.

As he rode, heading out for the line camp which he had left the previous day, he fell to wondering about Forlan. Somehow, he doubted Callaghan's idea of the man. He had met up with more than a score of such men; avaricious, desperate for power and influence, ready to trample down anyone who stood between them and their goal.

He had asked Lawson to accompany him out to the camp, feeling within his bones that if the pattern of the past few months were to be repeated, those rustlers would strike again at the herd — and soon. He wanted to be on hand when that happened. But the other had declined, merely saying that he had some unfinished business to attend to. Lando had half-guessed what the business might entail, knew that the other was just ripe for riding back into Mendaro and facing it out with Forlan and the sheriff. But although he had debated whether to ride with the other, he had finally decided against it. After all, he was not Lawson's keeper.

The restless wind moved through the brown mesquite on either side and set the stiff blades crackling with an eerie sound that gradually began to eat at his nerves. Topping a low rise, he stared off to the south. Here there was only desolation, a flat expanse of brown and yellow, an emptiness, with somewhere in the distance the Mexico border, a refuge for all of the riff-raff in the country. Once across that invisible line, they were safe from the law.

Threading his way through deep crevasses with their sides littered with huge boulders, thrown up in some past geological age, he came upon a long stretch of ground where the grass petered out, leaving only shale and stone preponderating. Here he was forced to move more slowly, shading his eyes against the full glare of the sun.

By noon, he was still in the rocky terrain, probing the territory around him. He judged that he was now very close to the southernmost limits of the Flying Y spread. Reining in by a small stream, he slaked his thirst and let the stallion drink its fill. Squatting in the shade of an overhanging ledge, he listened tautly to the stillness that lay like a blanket all about him. For a brief moment, he thought he detected the disturbing echo of hoofs in the distance, half-rose to his feet, then remained where he was, trying to pick out the sound more clearly. Presently, however, the sound died and it was difficult to tell whether he had really heard it or merely imagined it. Nothing moved now and even the wind had died away, leaving only the oppressive heat and silence.

Big Jet, suddenly impatient, pawed the muddy ground at the stream bank. Getting to his feet, Brad moved over, made to swing up into the saddle, then paused. Suddenly, from out of the rocky ledges perhaps a mile away there came a brief, brilliant flash of light. Brad froze in his tracks. A moment later, the flash came again and this time, he was able to pick out its position almost exactly, up among the high ridges which overlooked the wide stretch of pasture leading off in the direction of the line camp.

For a moment, it puzzled him, then it came to him what it was. Someone was out there using a spyglass, the sunlight striking off the lens catching his eyes. He stiffened mechanically, then climbing swiftly into the saddle, pulling Big Jet back among the boulders.

Evidently the other was not aware of him, had been intent on watching something off in the distance and to his way of thinking, it could mean only one thing. Somebody was keeping an eye on the herd and it was certainly not one of the Flying Y crew.

He rode for the best part of three-quarters of a mile, swinging in around the watcher's position before dismounting and going forward on foot the rest of the way. Climbing a steep side littered with boulders and knife-edged pieces of shale, he came out on a wide plateau, wriggled forward on his belly to the very edge, then peered down into the sun thrown shadows. There was very little to see among the rocks and even less to hear. The stillness pressed down on him from all sides, thick and enveloping. Waiting, he felt a vague prickling of imminent danger, but there was nothing to tell from which direction it might come, nor when.

Then his straining ears brought faint sounds from the distance. He made out the soft clink of metal against rock, muted but distinct — the scrape of a boot on the ground. Easing himself back, he moved off to his right, still circling around, his hand close to the butt of the pearl-handled Colt at his hip. The man he was hunting had certainly made the best use of cover, was well hidden even from behind. Lifting his gaze as he moved up through the rocks, he made out the faint, dark smudge of grey-brown in the far distance, knew that it was part of the Flying Y herd. Wherever the watcher was, he would have to be in line with it if he was to see anything at all. Using the distant herd as a sight, he moved a few more yards, then raised his head slowly, an inch at a time.

For a moment, he saw nothing

immediately below him, then his eye caught a faint movement some twenty yards away. A pair of legs protruded from behind an upthrusting boulder and he let his breath go between his teeth in a faint sigh of relief. Maybe just a lone scout, keeping an eye on the herd, ready to report back to the others wherever they might be; probably still a mile or so south of the border, out of reach.

He thinned his lips grimly. Slipping the Colt from leather, he moved noiselessly down the shale-strewn slope, picking his way carefully so as not to alert the other. The man was obviously still intent on spying on the herd, for he made no movement as Brad advanced on him.

Stepping out from behind a rock, Brad levelled the Colt on the other's prone figure, said thinly: 'Just stay quite still, friend, or I'll let you have it in the back.'

He saw the other stiffen abruptly, heard him mutter a harsh curse under his breath. The spyglass rested on a low wall of rock in front of him. Bending swiftly, Brad jerked the two weapons from the man's holsters and tossed them away, then took a step back.

'All right! On your feet!'

Slowly, the other complied, turning to face him. He was a heavily-set black-bearded man with a rusty-coloured scar along one cheek which gave him a permanent leer.

'Just what is this?' demanded the other thickly. He eyed Brad with a malevolent stare.

'Reckon I could ask you the same thing. This is Flying Y land, not open range. And to my way of reckonin', a man spyin' out a herd is up to no good. My guess is that you're one of the band who've been rustlin' this beef for some time now. Guess Jeb Callaghan will want to meet you.'

'Yeah? And supposin' that I don't want to meet him?' There was a note of confidence in the other's tone.

Brad shrugged. 'You can come

quietly, or slung over a saddle. Makes little difference to me.'

'That's where you're wrong' The other shifted his glance slightly, stared over Brad's shoulder. 'I'd drop that gun if I were you. There's a rifle trained on your back from the rocks right this minute.'

Before Brad could speak, the faint clatter of loose stones behind him, made the small hairs on the nape of his neck ruffle. He cursed himself inwardly for not remembering that faint sound of hoofs which he had heard in the canyon a little way back. So there were two of them, and like a blind fool, he had walked right into their trap.

'Better do as Miguel says,' said a hard voice at his back.

Reluctantly he dropped the Colt into the dirt, lifted his hands slowly to shoulder level. A further movement and the second man came into view on his left, the Winchester trained on his chest. Brad felt fear freeze his muscles. Both men were half-breeds and he knew he could expect no mercy at their hands.

'What do we do with the hombre, Miguel?' asked the man with the rifle.

The other glanced about him for a long moment before replying. Then he said harshly: 'There are plenty of places here where a body can be hidden until the coyotes get it. But before he dies, he can answer some questions that have been botherin' me. Then he'll die real slow.' There was a leering smile on the man's face, but no mirth showed in it and the cold bleakness in his eyes reminded Brad of a rattler about to strike.

Out of the corner of his eye, he watched the man with the rifle. The two men were now cocksure, confident that they had him dead to rights, that he would make no sudden move that might bring about his instant demise. The man came a little closer, his finger hard against the trigger, thrusting out with the long barrel until it struck against Brad's chest.

'Get movin' over into the rocks, amigo.'

Slowly, not taking his glance off the other, Brad half-turned as if to obey, shuffled his feet forward, deliberately dragging them in the dirt. The men grinned as Brad half staggered, his foot apparently slipping on one of the treacherous rocks. A fraction of a second later, the smile vanished as Brad acted. As swiftly as a striking snake, his right leg lashed out, catching the other behind one knee. At the same moment, he swung up with his arm, hitting the rifle barrel aside, twisting as he did so. The gun went off with a savage blast that almost deafened him and he felt the hot, scorching touch of burnt powder on his side, stinging even through the shirt.

With a startled oath, the other tried to swing the gun, yelling loudly to his companion. Without his guns, there was nothing to fear from the other at the moment. The half-breed, still gripping the Winchester, came up from a half crouch, his face exposed for half a second. Without pausing to think, Brad let go with a solid right to the other's jaw. Gasping, the gunhawk went back, blood spurting from his mouth where a tooth had gashed through the lower lip. His knees began to buckle as if unable to support his weight but with an effort, he fought himself upright, moving in with a grim, deadly purpose, now gripping the Winchester by the barrel, swinging it like a club at Brad's head.

Ducking savagely, Brad felt the wind of the gunbutt pass his face. Then he hurled himself forward, the crown of his head catching the man in the midriff, knocking all of the wind out of him. Clutching at his stomach, the other staggered back against the rocks, his body doubled up in agony. From the edge of his vision, Brad glimpsed the second man diving for his gun which lay in the dirt a few feet away.

Lunging forward, he kicked hard at the other's head, felt the toe of his boot slice against the man's ear. Then the half-breed's outstretched fingers clasped around the Colt. Before he could lift it, Brad's heel came down hard on the back of his hand. Uttering a wild yelp of pain, the man fell over on to his side, grabbing for his wrist.

Before he could move again, Brad had snatched up the gun, swinging it to cover the smaller man who now pushed himself away from the rocks, the Winchester already swinging around. Twisting, Brad jerked up the Colt and squeezed off a single shot. There was a brief puff of white dust from the front of the outlaw's shirt. Driven backward by the impact of the lead striking deep within his body, the man hung for a long moment against the rock face, arms and legs spread wide in an attitude of crucifixion. Then the life went swiftly out of him and he folded limply forward, crashing on to his face in the dirt, the rifle falling from nerveless fingers.

As he half turned, he heard the other man scrabbling in the shale. Hands fastened themselves around Brad's ankles as the other jerked hard with all of his strength, knowing now that he was fighting for his life. Caught off balance, Brad went down, his neck and shoulders hitting the ground, sending agony lancing through his upper body. Half-dazed, he saw the other get to his feet, breathing hard. There was blood on the side of his head where Brad's boot had raked across the flesh, tearing it to the bone.

He knew what was coming, knew that the other was a dirty fighter, brought up in a hard school. Lurching forward, the man dropped on to Brad's stomach with his knees. Grinning, he shifted his weight a little, edging forward, hands reaching for Brad's throat, clamping around his windpipe. Inexorably, he began to squeeze, exerting all of his strength, eyes narrowed down to slits, his breath coming in harsh, wheezing gasps through his open mouth.

Desperately, Brad clawed at the other's sinewy wrists, striving to pull the throttling hands away from his throat. Red sparks danced in front of his eyes as he struggled to draw air into his heaving lungs. He knew that somehow, he had to break that hold soon or perish. Gradually, the pressure increased. His throat felt raw, on fire with the strain. Already, the blackness of unconsciousness came seeping out of the rocks to engulf him completely.

With a supreme effort, Brad closed his mind to the panic which threatened to gain the upper hand. Concentrating all of his strength in his legs, he twisted them abruptly, bringing them up behind the gunhawk's neck, hooking his toes beneath the outthrusting chin. With the last of his fading strength, he jerked his legs back, felt the stranglehold relax as the other fell away.

Clutching at his bruised throat, Brad heaved himself to his feet, swaying on legs that seemed like jelly. At that moment he was in no condition to protect himself, but through his blurred vision, he saw that the other lay slumped against a small outcrop of rock, unmoving. Going forward, he went down on one knee. The half-breed was unconscious, breathing stertoriously.

Gradually, he felt his strength returning. Whistling up Big Jet, he heaved the unconscious man into the saddle, swung up behind him and rode down into the stretching grasslands.

There were three men at the line camp when he arrived there half an hour later. Brad recognized them as Kernahan, Winter and Ephraim. Kernahan came forward and took the unconscious gunhawk down, stretching him out on the ground.

'Trouble?' he asked, staring up at Brad.

The other gave a terse nod. 'Bumped into these two hombres a few miles back. This one had a spyglass, watchin' the herd. The other jumped me.'

'What about him?'

'He's dead.' Brad went over to the cabin with Kernahan trailing after him. Taking the coffee kettle off the stove, he poured himself a cup, drank it down gratefully. When he had finished, he said harshly: 'How many men do you have here?'

'Seven, including those out with the herd right now. Why?'

'From what I saw back there, I figure that those Mexes intend makin' another raid pretty soon. Maybe tonight. Those two half-breeds weren't out there for the sake of their health. When they don't report back to the main force, the others will know something's wrong. They'll try to hit us before we're ready for 'em; before we can get more men out from the ranch.'

Kernahan whistled thinly through his teeth. 'Seven of us won't stand much chance against that bunch.'

'Eight,' Brad corrected. 'But fore-warned is forearmed. So long as we're ready, we might have a chance.'

'You don't know these gunhawks. They can muster twenty or thirty men.'

'Then it's up to us to even the odds a little.' Brad splashed more coffee into the cup, sipped the scalding liquid slowly, face furrowed in concentration. 'We're out in the open here. They can attack from any direction they choose. We've got to find a better defensive position before nightfall.'

Kernahan rubbed his chin. 'What's wrong with this place? At least we'd have plenty of cover behind the walls.'

'The walls are thick enough, but this roof is timber. They only need to fire it and we'd be roasted alive. Better try and get up into the hills and drive the herd there. I spotted a narrow pass on my way here that looked ideal for holdin' off these hombres.'

Kernahan nodded. 'I'll get word to the rest of the boys right away.'

3

Night Attack!

It became increasingly plain to Brad during the next few hours that if a showdown came they would have the fight of their lives. Throughout the long, boiling afternoon, they had driven the reluctant herd over the edge of the grasslands and up into the narrow draw, flanked on either side by tall, virtually unscalable rocks. In spite of this advantage, there were obvious drawbacks to the place. The far end of the pass was a dead end, cut off by a sheer wall of rock rising to close on two hundred feet. If those cattle should be spooked, they could stampede out of the end of the draw and be scattered to hell and beyond before the men had a chance to stop them.

But it was the best they could do in

the short time they had available. He now felt more certain than ever that the raiders would strike once darkness fell. By early evening, the herd was in place, milling around on this unfamiliar ground and obviously nervous. They ate a cold meal of unheated beans, chewed strips of tough jerky washed down with water from their canteens. To have lit a fire would have been a dead give-away of their position.

As darkness settled, they paired off, taking up their places among the saw-toothed outcrops. Brad had taken the precaution of putting two men up on top of the rock wall which shut off the end of the canyon in case any of the outlaws attacked from that end, with the rest of the men on either side of the deep canyon covering their flanks.

Brad settled down in the darkness beside Flint, the Flying Y foreman, listening to the wind as it lifted and moaned down the length of the draw, rising and falling with a monotonous regularity, like the voice of a lost soul in the distance. The minutes began to drag and waiting became a strain. Lighting a cigarette, he pulled the smoke deep into his lungs, feeling it bring a little warmth back into his chilled body. The night air was dry but bitterly cold and he flexed his fingers as he smoked.

'You really figure they'll hit us tonight?' Flint spoke softly out of the shrouding darkness, only the faintly glowing tip of his cigarette picking out the details of his features beneath the wide-brimmed hat.

'They'll come,' Brad said with an even sureness. 'They know by now that we've got those two men and they can't afford to wait any longer.'

Eleven o'clock came and went. Shifting his weight a little as the hard rock pressed into his bones, Brad moved to the tip of the short drop-off and stared out into the darkness. Nothing moved as far as he could see apart from the uneasy milling of the herd as the longhorns bedded down for the night. If they start making any sound at all, they'll give us away, he thought tensely.

Midnight and still the quietness was absolute all about them. Flint got stiffly to his feet, brought his heel down sharply on the butt of his cigarette. 'They'd have been here before now if they was comin',' he grunted hoarsely. 'If they've headed for the camp and found us gone, could be they've decided to hightail it back over the border rather than spend the rest of the night searching miles of empty pasture.'

Brad pursed his lips thoughtfully. What the other said was quite possible, but somehow he didn't think so. These men evidently worked to some kind of plan and he tried to put himself in their place. Checking the chambers of the Colt, he thrust it back into its holster, then froze as a faint drumming from the south-east reached him. Grabbing Flint's arm, he pulled him down among the rocks. The other had picked out the sound too for he raised his head, probing the dimness.

'They're headed this way,' the foreman muttered in a low tone. 'Could be they've guessed what we've done.'

Keeping his own counsel, Brad edged away, crawling over the needle-sharp rocks until he reached a small hollow from where he could peer between a wide Vee-shaped notch. He held motionless, barely breathing as he spotted the faint cloud of dust off in the distance. By now, the rest of the Flying Y crew would have heard the sound of the oncoming riders and would be ready.

Five minutes later, he could make out the shadowy shapes of the individual riders, strung out in a loose bunch as they converged on the draw. Almost certainly they had been at the line camp and then trailed the herd to this point. The blast of a rifle jerked his taut nerves even though he had been expecting it. In the near distance, the outlaws swung away, scattering for cover.

Pressing himself hard against the

rocks, Brad realized that not all of the band had ridden for cover. A small group were spurring their mounts directly for the end of the canyon, crouching low in the saddle, firing as they came on. Lead slashed among the rocks, ricocheted off the unyielding surface with the shrill whine of tortured metal.

Slightly below him, Flint worked the lever of his carbine, sending a stream of shots into the rushing riders. Three men toppled from their saddles in almost as many seconds, but still the others came on, disregarding the withering hail of fire which poured into them. Brad emptied his Colt into the charging men, knew there was no time in which to reload before those still in the saddle entered the draw. If they once started stampeding those steers all hell would be let loose. Scrambling to his feet, he moved to the edge of the drop-off, saw one of the outlaws spurring his mount on into the mouth of the canyon, waited tensely until the other was level with him, then launched himself out into space. He hit the rider squarely on the back, knocking him out of the saddle. Locked together, they crashed to the hard ground with Brad uppermost.

The outlaw twisted like a cat, strove to rise to his feet, then collapsed inertly as the butt of the Colt caught him a savage blow on the top of the skull. The criss-crossing lances of flame from the rocks wove a deadly curtain of lead over his head as he crouched there over the fallen rustler. It did not take him long to realize that the outlaws were now moving in from all directions, advancing boldly, making use of every scrap of cover, sure that with their superiority in numbers they had complete control over the situation.

One of the Flying Y crew high in the rocks suddenly screamed in mortal agony, seemed to leap up and out from the rock face, his body turning over and over as it fell. He hit the hard-packed ground less than ten yards from where

Brad crouched thumbing fresh shells into his gun, and lay still.

More riders appeared at the entrance to the canyon. Brad saw the stilettos of blue-crimson flame from their drawn guns in the split second that he threw himself sideways, heard the lead strike the rocky ground within inches of his body.

He was thankful for the deep shadows within the canyon where the high walls shut out the moonlight which was beginning to flood the prairie. Aiming swiftly, he returned the fire of the riders, kicking spurs into their horses' flanks, pushing them forward into the draw. There was no doubting their intention. They meant to prod the already nervous herd into instant action, to cut out a sizeable bunch and drive them out, almost certainly heading them south for the border. Once they got them across that line dividing Texas from Mexico, there would be not a hope in hell of getting any of them back.

Out of the corner of his eye, he saw the outlaws swinging their mounts around the side of the herd, the skittish cattle already brought to a high pitch by the sound of gunfire echoing and racketing within the confining walls of the canyon. A dark shape moved across his vision. He had a brief glimpse of a white face under the sombrero, then the man threw up his arms and dropped sideways as Brad fired. One foot caught in the stirrup, the man was dragged by his onrushing mount, his head bouncing on the uneven ground.

In the darkness, it was impossible to see all of the outlaws. By now, their mounts had blended with the dark, shapeless mass of the herd. More gunfire came from the rocks and he judged that at least half of the gang had been killed. But they still outnumbered the Flying Y crew and some of the lead had taken its inevitable toll of the defenders.

Pressing his back hard against the cold rock, he sent another shot at a running shade, cursed inwardly as he realized that he had missed. The night was filled with the din of gunfire and then, suddenly, without any warning, a fresh sound reached Brad's ears. It was a sound both familiar and frightening. The rumble of tons of beef on the move. The rustlers had somehow succeeded in cutting off a large bunch of cattle. Now they had moved in between it and the main herd. In the distance, he made out the riders swinging in their mounts behind the steers, firing their guns close to the heads of the half-crazed animals. The ground began to tremble under his feet as close on half a thousand head of cattle turned and began to stream in a relentless, irresistible mass towards the wide opening of the draw.

It was worse than useless to try to stop them. Down here on the ground, he recognized his own personal danger. Dimly, he was aware of the black tide which came sweeping in his direction. A minute, perhaps less, lay between him and a hideous end, trampled underfoot by those pounding hooves. Desperately, all thought of the outlaw band forgotten, he cast about him for some way up into the rocks.

Now that his eyes had grown accustomed to the gloom, he saw the narrow defile perhaps twenty yards away. Pushing himself away from the canyon wall he began to run, knowing that death was only a short distance behind. Feet slipping in the treacherous shale, he ran as he had never run before. Once he fell, dropped on to his hands and knees, heaved himself back on to his feet with a convulsive movement, feeling the warm stickiness of blood on his left hand where a needle point of rock had gashed through the flesh, slicing it almost to the bone. But the pain was forgotten in the fear of the moment.

A steer crashed past him, the pointed horns less than an inch from his shoulder. The rest were only scant yards behind, plunging forward in a mad rush. His heart thumping against his ribs, his breath harsh and hot in his throat, he came upon the rocky defile, urged himself up into it, clawing for hand holds. Moments later, he was comparatively safe on a narrow ledge, gripping the rocks with stiff fingers. Below him, the relentless tide surged past in a fury of sound.

Slowly, the sound of the stampede died into the distance, leaving only the atrophying echoes ringing in his ears, his eardrums quivering under that mighty onslaught of noise. Gasping air down into his chest, he pushed himself into a sitting position, stared down into the canyon. The rest of the herd were still in position, milling around aimlessly. But it still needed only an untoward sound or movement to set them off also.

Cautiously, every nerve and fibre in his body stretched to breaking point, he let himself down on to the canyon floor. Off in the distance, the muted rumble of the steers dwindled into a dull roll of sound. Above him, a final volley of gunfire crashed out — and then there was silence.

Flint came clambering down amid a shower of small stones. He eyed Brad speculatively. 'You all right?' he asked thinly, voice edged with tension.

'Sure, but it was a near thing. Better check how many head they got away with. And how many men we lost.'

'You figure we ought to go out after 'em?'

Brad shook his head decisively. 'Not much point in that. They'll have them across the border into Mexico in less than an hour. We'd never catch up with 'em in time.'

'At least we dropped a few of the critters.' The other jerked a horny thumb in the direction of the inert bodies a few yards away.

'Get a few of the boys to tote 'em into Mendaro and hand the bodies over to the sheriff.'

A faint gust of surprise flashed over the other's face. 'What good would that do? They're only ready for the coroner. Better to bury 'em here and have done with it.'

'Maybe so. But I figure we might push Kerdy out into the open; see which way he jumps. My guess is that some of these men at least have been hangin' around town these past few weeks, keepin' their eyes and ears open. Might be one or two of 'em will be recognized.'

Flint's lips twisted back in a mirthless grin of understanding. 'I'll get a few of the boys on to that right away.' Turning his head, he stared towards the southern horizon. 'Reckon those hombres won't be comin' back again tonight anyway.'

Two hours later, a rough count had been made of the remaining steers in the canyon. Almost five hundred head had been stampeded out of the main herd. Two men had been killed during the attack and three others wounded, one of them so badly that it was only a matter of time before he died.

★　★　★

The stifling heat of high noon overran the spacious office, filled the corners with a glare of light that spilled in through the wide windows. Jess Forlan got heavily to his feet and went across to the window, lowered the shade impatiently, then wiped the sweat from his forehead with a silk handkerchief. Outside, the street was almost deserted. A mangy cur loped across the sun-baked earth, found a narrow stretch of shadow beneath an overhanging awning and sank down gratefully into it, its tongue lolling from its panting jaws. Few of the townsfolk were out. This was the siesta time, a custom borrowed of necessity from the Mexicans. As he made to move back into the room, he stopped. A solitary rider was approaching from the far end of the street, a man who sat slumped forward in the saddle, riding slowly but with a singleness of purpose which immediately attracted his attention. A moment later, as the man lifted his head, Forlan recognized him. He moved to one side of the window, watched as Dave Lawson reined up immediately outside the building, dropped from the saddle and looped the reins over the rail. The rancher threw a quick glance up towards the window, hesitated for a moment, glancing up and down the street, then moved towards the door.

Brow furrowed, Forlan moved back towards his desk. Opening the drawer, he took out the small Derringer, checked it, then thrust it into his belt. Sitting back in his chair, he waited for the knock to come to the door. When it came, he called out: 'Come in, Lawson.'

The door opened slowly and the rancher stepped into the room, blinking a little against the glare of the sunlight.

'Shut the door,' Forlan said quietly.

Lawson hesitated, then closed the door, backed against it for a moment, eyes flicking around the room, then he suddenly straightened, hitched the gunbelt a little higher about his middle with a curiously jerky movement.

'All right, what do you want? Make it quick, I'm busy.'

'You know damn well what I'm here for, Forlan,' gritted the other thinly. 'My wife was killed by that murderin' bunch of half-breeds you sent to burn down the ranch. I'm here to make sure that you pay for her death. You're not worth anythin' more than a slug in the belly.'

Forlan recognized the look on the other's face, sat forward behind the desk. He shook his head. 'If you think I was responsible for that, then you're mistaken. It was none of my doin'.'

'Don't lie to me, Forlan. So long as I paid you that money, there was no trouble. Then when I stopped, you sent those men to make sure that I was finished.'

'That's not true.' Forlan realized that the other had worked himself up into such a pitch that he would do anything. 'I'll admit that I promised protection to those ranchers who paid for it. That's business. But as for cold-blooded murder, that's not my way at all.'

'It's no go, Forlan. You can swear that you're innocent on a stack of Bibles but I still won't believe you. I know your sort. You sit here behind that desk like some bloated spider, spinning your web throughout the whole territory, giving orders to those killers, knowin' that they'll be carried out and nobody can prove a thing against you. But this is the end of the trail for you.'

'You intend to shoot me down in cold blood?' Forlan gave a quick shake of his head. 'That ain't your way, Lawson, and you know it. I don't carry a gun. Shoot me and you'll have this whole town on your neck before you can reach the street. They'll take you outside of town and stretch your neck on the end of a rope within minutes.'

'You reckon that bothers me now that Ellie's dead?' There was a rising inflection in the other's tone which Forlan recognized at once. He saw now that the other cared little what happened to him so long as he took the man he judged to be responsible with him. If he was to save his own life, he would have to play this thing more carefully than anything else in his life.

'Before you do anythin' you might regret, stop and think. Kill me and those men who did the killin' will go scott free. I'm tellin' you again that I had nothin' whatever to do with it. It's Mendoza you want, not me, and he happens to be in the Golden Ace saloon right now. Why don't you and me take a walk down there and you can get the truth out of him? If he claims I paid him to burn your place and kill your wife, then you can still put a bullet in me if you're so inclined.'

As he spoke, he kept his glance fixed on the rancher's face, at the same time, easing his right hand down towards the edge of the desk, just above the spot where the weight of the Derringer pressed into his belly. 'Now what d'you say? That's a fair enough offer to my mind and — '

There was a heavy step on the stairway outside the door. Lawson jerked sharply, then pulled the Colt from his holster, levelled it at the banker. 'You expectin' anyone, Forlan?'

'No one in particular.'

A knock sounded on the door, loud and imperative.

'All right. Tell 'em to step inside. And remember, a bullet can travel quicker than you can give any order.'

Forlan swallowed thickly, acutely aware of the other's finger tight on the trigger. 'Come in,' he called harshly.

The door swung open and Sheriff Kerdy came bustling into the office. His startled gaze took in the tableau at the desk and for a split second his right hand started for the gun at his waist, then he froze as Lawson snapped: 'You go for that gun, Sheriff, and Forlan dies.'

'He means it, Kerdy.' Forlan pushed himself upright in the chair as Lawson swung around so that he could watch both of the men. 'Better do like he says.'

Kerdy drew back his lips, but kept his hand well away from his gun as he stepped into the room, his face tight with wrath.

'Close that door,' Lawson commanded thinly. 'Then step over here and drop that gunbelt — real slow.'

Kerdy did not move. Lawson frowned, moved closer to the banker and placed the tip of the barrel right up against the other's ear. Forlan winced and a fresh beading of sweat broke out on his forehead and upper lip. 'I told you to do as he says, Sheriff.' There was a faint quaver in his voice. 'He means it.'

Reluctantly, the lawman loosened the buckle, let the heavy gunbelt fall with a clatter to the floor. There was the bleak promise of death in the depths of his eyes as he lifted his head to stare across at the rancher.

'This is the second score I've got to settle with you, Mister,' he growled. 'I won't forget it.'

'Right now, you're in no position to make any threat, Kerdy. I came here to kill the man who arranged to have my place burnt to the ground and who's responsible for my wife's murder. I reckon I've found him. You're just in time to witness the execution.'

'I've already told him it was none of my doin'. That Mendoza is the man responsible and that he's down in the saloon,' interjected Forlan hurriedly. 'You can vouch for that, Kerdy.' He shot the lawman a quick glance, making a faint movement with the fingers of his left hand, out of sight of the rancher.

Kerdy caught himself abruptly, nodded quickly. 'That's right. If you want him, he's right where Forlan says he is.'

'Then if he's here in town, why haven't you arrested him? You know damn well that Mex is behind all of this rustlin' and killin'. It's your job to get him.'

Kerdy's Adam's apple bobbed up and down for a moment. Then he said tautly: 'Knowin' that he's the man and provin' it are two different things, as you ought to know. If the law is to be upheld, then I've got to have concrete proof of his guilt. But you seem so all-fired sure of it, then do somethin' about it.'

'And what will you be doin'?'

Kerdy gave a nonchalant shrug of his shoulders. 'Nothin', I reckon. You rid this territory of a man like Mendoza and I reckon you'll be doin' the folk of Mendaro a good turn. My hands are tied. Yours ain't. You got cause to kill him.' He shuffled his feet uncertainly for a moment. 'A man's got the right to protect himself accordin' to my book.'

Lawson hesitated, then reached a sudden decision. He moved back a couple of paces. 'All right. Both of you move out ahead of me.' He waved the Colt menacingly. 'No! You leave your gunbelt where it is, Kerdy. I don't aim to be shot in the back.'

Kerdy straightened up abruptly in the act of bending down to reach for his guns. A deep flush spread over his face at the implication behind the other's words and for a moment, the look of action showed on his face. Then he thought better of it, turned and moved towards the door with the portly figure of the banker close behind.

Watchfully, Lawson moved after them, down the stairs and out on to the sun-hazed boardwalk, the Colt still in his fist. There was the feeling deep inside him that he ought to have killed Forlan while he had had the chance up there in the office, but he ignored it. The street was empty as the three men walked slowly towards the saloon. From inside, there came the sound of harsh voices and the faint, tinny sound of the piano. With a jerk of the Colt, he motioned the two men to precede him. Kerdy stepped up to the batwing doors, thrust them open with the flat of his hand and went inside.

Alert for any treachery, Lawson moved in. There were several men in the saloon, some seated at the tables, others ranged along the low bar. Lawson noticed that several of the men were Mexicans, with a sprinkling of cowpokes. For a moment, seeing all of these men standing there, he felt a little tremor of fear pass through him as the full enormity of the situation hit him forcibly. Until that moment, the dull anger in his mind, the sense of utter loss when everything he had held dear had been taken from him, had dominated everything. Now he realized, quite suddenly, that death might lie close.

He saw the men at the bar turn to stare at him, saw the card players at the tables stop their games, swivelling in their chairs. Behind the bar, the florid-faced bartender moved back a couple of paces, his eyes darting to the spot where he undoubtedly kept the scattergun ready in case of trouble such as was about to erupt at any moment. Then all feeling left him. The hand which held the gun became steady and his voice was oddly calm as he said loudly so that everyone could hear: 'Which of you polecats is Mendoza?'

One of the men pushed himself away from the bar, threw a sideways glance at the rest of the men ranged on either side of him, his hands hovering close to the twin butts of the guns at his sides. His eyes were narrowed down to mere slits.

'I'm Mendoza,' he said thinly.

'Then I guess you're the coyote I'm lookin' for.'

'Nobody calls Jose Mendoza that, not even a man with a gun in his hand,' said the other, his voice like the lash of a whip in the room. Even as he spoke, his hand slashed downward in a blur of motion, the guns seeming to jump into his clawing fingers. Flame burst from them and gunsmoke swirled about him. In spite of his speed, Lawson got off the first shot, but even as he squeezed the trigger, Kerdy slashed out with his right hand, knocking him hard on the wrist. His slug went high, smashing into the glass mirror behind the bar, sending a shower of glittering fragments over the counter. The thunder of gunfire seemed to shake the building to its very foundations, then it died slowly away and a deep silence settled over the saloon.

At the bar, Mendoza slowly sheathed the twin guns, stood for a moment staring across the room, then turned back to where his drink stood on the bar. Near the door, Lawson coughed painfully, then bent in two, dropped his gun into the sprinkling of sawdust at his feet. He took a short, hesitant step forward, tried to lift his head to stare round at the man who had spoilt his aim, a man who stood with a vicious grin on his face. Then a convulsive shudder ran through the rancher. Blood trickled down his chin as he sagged suddenly, crumpled and toppled over on to his face, one arm twisted beneath him. He stirred just once after he collapsed, a brief twitching of his legs, then lay still. From under him, a slowly widening red stain ran into the sawdust which soaked it up avidly.

Without turning his head, Mendoza said; 'Just who was that fool, Kerdy?'

'Fellow named Lawson. You and some of your men razed his ranch a day or two ago.'

'Seems to me like you need some law and order in this town, *amigo*, when men can go around with drawn guns like that.'

There came the rush of feet on the boardwalk outside and a small crowd of men burst into the saloon. Whirling on his feet, Kerdy roared: 'It's all over now, folks. There ain't much to see. This hombre drew first.'

For a long moment, the townsfolk stared down at the man on the floor with bulging eyes, then one said tensely: 'It's Dave Lawson.'

'He came here lookin' for trouble — and found it,' muttered Kerdy. 'Plenty of witnesses to say that it was a fair fight.'

'One of you men fetch the coroner.'

Forlan gave the order with a curious expression on his fleshy features. For a moment, he looked as though he were going to be sick. Then he stepped over the body on the floor and pushed his way through the men near the door, going out into the boardwalk, where he stood for a long moment drawing the hot noon air down into his lungs. Then he made his way slowly back towards his office, slumped down in the chair behind the desk and poured himself out a glass of whisky tossing it down in a single gulp.

★   ★   ★

Brad dropped his hat into a chair that stood beside the door took another one for himself and stared across the room at Callaghan. The other was standing at the open window, his hands clasped tightly behind his back, his face turned away from Brad. As the other maintained his heavy silence, Brad took the opportunity to look around the room, seeing it clearly for the first time. There was, he noticed a handsome carpet on the floor, the pile thick beneath his boots, half a dozen carved chairs to match the big desk and a long bookcase ranged along one wall with a picture over the wide hearth. All in all, the place was furnished in a more pretentious style than any he had seen before. Quite obviously, in spite of the troubles which the other claimed to have experienced in the past few months, he was still sufficiently well endowed with money to live in comparative luxury.

Turning abruptly, the other lowered himself into the ornate chair behind the desk, fingers clasped in front of him, his face devoid of any emotion.

'You say that they got away with close to five hundred head last night?' he muttered finally.

'That's right. We managed to save most of the herd but there were more'n twenty of them. We never had much of a chance. By now, those cattle will be miles across the border.'

'And the crew?'

'We lost three men. One died early

this mornin',' replied Brad flatly.

'I see. And you're sure they were Mendoza's men?'

'In the darkness all men look alike. But I don't see who else it could have been.'

Callaghan drummed on the desk top with his fingers for a moment, lips pressed tightly over his teeth.

'I'm afraid I've got some bad news for you, Lando. Firstly, it wasn't Mendoza who hit my herd last night. Not unless he can be in two places at the same time. I've been informed that he was in Mendaro all day yesterday and last night. Most of his men seem to have been there with him.'

'That so? Then I reckon it just goes to bear out what I've been thinkin' for some time now. That those in authority in Mendaro either won't, or daren't, go against these killers. Seems they have the free run of the place.'

'Secondly,' put in the other almost as though he hadn't heard, 'your friend, Dave Lawson, was killed yesterday.

Sheriff Kerdy brought his body back here early this morning.'

Brad sat quite still in his chair for a long moment, staring at the other, his face tight. He had only known Lawson for a few days but he had grown to like the rancher. 'How did it happen?' he asked tautly.

'From what I've heard he pulled a gun on Forlan and the sheriff, forced them to go along to the Golden Ace saloon where he held a gun on Mendoza. There was a gunfight and Lawson was killed. That's all the information I have. I'm sorry.'

'And no doubt everybody in the saloon swore it was a fair fight,' Brad said viciously, bitterness edging his voice.

'That's the way of it. And — ' went on the other meaningly, ' — you won't get any of 'em to change their testimony. Most of 'em were Mendoza's men anyway.'

'All nice and easy.' Brad thrust himself to his feet and Callaghan felt a tiny shiver go through him as he stared up at the big man, saw the look on his features, the icy coldness at the back of his eyes. He said quietly:

'You figure on avengin' Lawson's death, Lando?'

'I had somethin' like that in mind.'

'Don't bother, otherwise you'll end up exactly as he did. Even forgettin' about Mendoza who's nothin' more than a killer, Forlan and Kerdy will involve you in murder no matter what you do. I've been around here long enough to know how those two work. Forlan deals in murder — it helps him get rid of any opposition and he makes it a means to an end, furthers his own interests. He has a knack of makin' incriminatin' evidence against anyone who stands in his way. All these men are in his pay — Kerdy, those deputies of his, half of the influential folk in town. And even if Kerdy doesn't come after you himself, there are the Vigilantes, so called decent citizens of Mendaro, who really do the undercover, dirty work for

Forlan. And just in case that don't work, then they arrange for some trigger-happy gunman from along the border to come into town, pick a gunfight and then shoot you down in the street or in the back from some dark alley.'

'I get the picture,' Brad spoke heavily, thoughtfully. 'But it ain't the first time I've come up against somethin' like this.'

'Maybe not. Maybe in the past you've always been faster with a gun than the next man. But there's always a first time when you come up against somebody just a shade faster and more cunning than you are. We've got a cemetery outside of town, full of men who figured they could beat another man to the draw.'

'Guess that's a chance I'll have to take,' Brad said coldly.

'Suit yourself, but don't say I didn't give you damn fair warnin'.' Callaghan scraped back his chair, got up, resting his knuckles on the desk. 'It'd be a pity to lose a good man, just when I figured I might be gettin' on top of all this trouble.'

Brad thinned his lips in a mirthless grin. 'You ain't lost me yet,' he countered. 'I'm plannin to do a heap more than Lawson did. I trust that you'll see to it that he gets a decent burial while I'm gone.'

'I'll do that much for you,' acknowledged the other sombrely. 'You want any of the boys to ride into town with you? Flint's a good man and the least he could do would be to stay undercover and watch your back if you do go up against any of these coyotes.'

Brad pondered that for a moment, then shook his head decisively. 'I'll do this chore better alone,' he said. 'So far only Kerdy knows what I look like.'

'And you want to keep it that way. I can't say I blame you. In a deadly game like this, you'll sure need all the edge you can get, believe me. Forlan is playin' for high stakes and he's got

too darn much to lose to let anythin'
stop him now.'

'I'll bear that in mind,' Brad promised. He picked up his hat, jammed it
hard on his head and made for the
door.

4

Manhunt

It was early evening as Brad entered one of the narrow alleys of Mendaro. He had left Big Jet tethered in a quiet side-street, knew that the well-trained animal would not stray far. Now he halted briefly, hesitantly, at the point where two alleys met at an angle. With a coming of evening, a slight breeze had sprung up, blowing off the distant mountains and there was a welcome coolness to the air which swirled about him, lifting tiny eddies of white dust. He sucked in a deep breath, felt it revive him after the long ride of the afternoon.

As he had swung around the edge of town, he had noticed that there was plenty of activity in the main street. There were long rows of horses tied up outside the bars and saloons and lights showing in all of the windows facing the street. As far as he was aware, his approach had gone unnoticed, but as Callaghan had said, this town was an uneasy sort of place, riddled with intrigue and murder and he could rely on nothing and nobody.

Cat-footing along the alley, skirting the piles of rubbish which lay strewn in every direction, he passed an empty grain store, reached the intersection with the main street and paused, glancing intently in both directions. He had come out some fifty yards from the Golden Ace saloon and on the opposite side of the street. In the floor of yellow light that spilled on to the boardwalk, he noticed that several of the horses outside the place had clearly come in from across the border.

That meant that Mendoza was almost certainly still in town, utterly sure of himself, knowing that nothing could possibly harm him here, that the law was as crooked as the men who ran the place. Stepping up on to the boardwalk, he pulled the brim of his hat a little further over his eyes, forcing himself to walk slowly. Only one man in town knew him, knew of his connection with Dave Lawson and unless he bumped into Kerdy unexpectedly, he was reasonably safe, just another trail rider.

Reaching a spot directly opposite the saloon, he leaned his shoulders against a wooden upright and made himself a cigarette. He had smoked too much during the long ride out from the Flying Y but a cigarette was useful in more ways than one and gave him the opportunity of looking the place over without making himself too conspicuous. Drawing the match down the post, he waved the flame over the tip of the cigarette and drew on it slowly.

Several silhouettes showed dark against the well-lit windows and the sound of raucous laughter drifted out to him on the cool air. Then, without any warning, a whisky bottle came sailing out over the top of the batwing doors and landed with a splintering crash against one of the posts. The laughter welled up to a crescendo and a moment later, a man came staggering out of the doors, arms flailing as he landed on his face in the dust.

Picking himself up, the other started to run blindly across the street in Brad's direction, throwing a frightened look over his shoulder as he ran. Brad noticed that the other's holsters were empty, caught a fragmentary glimpse of the white-whiskered face under the floppy hat. Seconds later, the doors were thrust open again and two men barged through, guns in their hands.

The fugitive had almost reached the boardwalk, only a few yards from where Brad stood. He heard the other's gasping breath, saw him sway for a moment, hanging on to a post to keep himself up. One of the watching gunhawks lifted his Colt, squeezed off a couple of shots, the flying lead kicking up tiny puffs of dust around the fugitive's feet. Then he moved out into the street, heading for the trembling man who suddenly pulled himself up on to the boardwalk, scrambled past Brad with an appealing look on his face and made for the dark mouth of a nearby alley, seeking shelter.

'You can't run far enough to get away,' yelled one of the men loudly. He sent a third shot after the fleeing figure.

The man had stopped at the wall, breathing hard, all of his strength apparently dissipated. He could obviously run no further. Grinning wolfishly, the two gunslingers closed in on him, raising their guns menacingly. Now there was a deliberateness, a curious coldness, about their actions and Brad knew that this time they did not intend to scare the other; this time they meant to finish him for good.

The leading man took a step forward to where his victim teetered in a half-crouch against the wall. His teeth showed whitely in the shadow of his face as he levelled the gun. The next instant, the Colt went flying from his smashed fingers, clattering on to the slatted boardwalk. Whirling, he turned to face the man who had fired the shot, his companion turning at the same time, a faint look of surprise on his coarse, grim features.

'Why you — '

'Better let that gun drop,' Brad said smoothly, very softly, 'or the next slug will go right between your eyes.'

The muscles in the man's jaw twitched violently. For a long moment he tried to stare Brad down, then something in the other's attitude struck through to him and with a savage curse, he released his hold on the gun.

'You two hombres get a kick out of shootin' up unarmed men?'

The others' mouths tightened into scowls. Neither spoke.

'What's wrong? Lost your tongues? I asked you a question.'

'Ain't none of your business what we do,' growled the man with the injured hand.

'Reckon I'm makin' it my business.' Brad took a couple of steps forward, moving easily. He flicked a quick look at the man who stood in the alley mouth, his eyes wide watching them. It was at that moment that the bigger man decided to make his play. Side-stepping, he threw himself at Brad, his right fist lashing out. Whirling, Brad let him come on, then swung the Colt in a short arc. It connected with a stunning blow on the side of the other's head, pitching him sideways. Without a moan, the other slumped against the edge of the boardwalk. His hat, torn from his head, went rolling along the street, finishing up in the gutter. Before his companion could make any move, the Colt was up again, covering him, Brad's finger taut on the trigger.

'Just try something,' he said thinly. 'It'll give me the greatest pleasure to plug you right here.'

Eyes blazing, clutching his shattered fingers, the other grunted: 'I don't know who you are, Mister. But I won't forget your face. One day — and soon — I'll meet up with you on even terms.'

'I can hardly wait,' Brad said nonchalantly. 'Now start back for the saloon.'

Slowly, the sullen gunhawk shuffled across the street, paused for a moment on the far side, then crashed in through the swing doors. Swiftly, Brad holstered the Colt, turned to the man crouching in the alley. The other gave him a quick glance, said harshly: 'You shouldn't have butted in like that, friend. Now you're in real trouble. Those two are real mean when they're riled. They won't wait until they've hunted you down and paid you in full for what you just did.'

'Like I said, I've got plenty of patience. Just who were they?'

'Reston and Crawley. They call themselves the Vigilantes. All that means is that they work for Forlan on the quiet.'

'I've heard of 'em,' Brad muttered grimly. He caught the other's arm and helped him back into the shadowed alley. 'You'd better find your bronc and get out of Mendaro before they decide to bring more of their kind to hunt you down.'

'Sure — and thanks, Mister. My name's Herb Thompson. I've got a small spread north of here. Any time you want a place or a job, just ride in.'

'Thanks. But I've already got a job with Jeb Callaghan at the Flying Y.' He hurried the other on as the man seemed intent on talking. At any moment, he knew that there would be a rush of men out of the saloon looking for them. 'Where's your mount?'

'Back there outside the saloon. No chance of reachin' it now. But don't worry none about me. I'll make out. You'd better watch your step if you're stayin' in town for the night.'

They reached the far end of the alley where it opened out on to a stretch of uneven, humped ground which, a couple of hundred yards further on, gave way to desert, Thompson made his way across it at a slow run, crouching down until he reached the smooth expanse of the desert. Brad watched him until he was gone from sight, then cut along a narrow passageway between two high fences. In the distance, he picked out the sound of loud voices coming from the direction of the street, guessed what it meant. Five minutes later, he was back in the main street, now to the west of the saloon. Further along, he saw the small knot of men near the boardwalk. Two of them were bent over the figure of the man he had knocked out.

Then another figure came striding out of an office and in a shaft of light Brad recognised Sheriff Kerdy. The other's booming voice reached him in the silence which had suddenly fallen over the group.

'You say that this hombre cut in on you while you was goin' after Thompson?'

The man with the injured hand said something which Brad could not catch, but Kerdy's reply was plain enough as he turned, raising his voice to address the men.

'This sounds like that hombre who rode in with Lawson a few days ago. He carries a pearl-handled Colt. You shouldn't have any difficulty recognizin' him. Spread out in threes and search the town. If you spot him, bring him back to my office.'

'Dead or alive, Sheriff?' called one of the men.

'Anyway you like. Makes no difference to me.' Kerdy hitched his gunbelt a little higher about his middle, then sauntered back in the direction of his office.

Brad thinned down his lips. Evidently the so-called lawman did not intend risking his own hide, but was content to leave it to the others. Turning his head quickly, Brad peered about him, seeking out the concealing shadows as a plan began to form in his mind. Doubled-over, he ran across the street, threw himself down behind a water trough, lay quite still for a moment, then wriggled back, still out of sight of the bunch of men. He doubted if any of them would bother going after Thompson now that they had transferred their attention to him.

Thrusting himself to his feet, he moved around the edge of the building, worked his way along the wall until he came upon the narrow ladder which led up towards the upper storey from the outside. Hand over hand, he pulled himself up to the point where the ladder stopped just outside one of the upper windows. There was a narrow ledge which would enable anyone to gain entry, but this was not his intention. Just above him, the roof jutted out for perhaps a couple of feet and by stretching himself up to his full height, he succeeded in hooking his fingers around the edge. Letting go with his feet, he dangled in mid air for a long moment, his full weight on his arms, the muscles of his shoulders creaking with the strain.

Sucking in a deep breath, he began to swing himself from side to side. Then his right foot caught on the overhanging gutter and he shifted all of his concentration into maintaining a hold on it. For what seemed an eternity, he hung there, summoning all of his strength into one last, desperate heave. Moments later he was lying flat on the sloping portion of the roof, drawing air down into his heaving lungs, his heart pumping madly against his ribs.

Down below, he heard the shouts of the men in the main street as they formed themselves into small groups. Pushing himself upright, he worked his way precariously along the roof, came to the far end. Some ten feet separated him from the next building. It was a short enough distance to jump, but the opposite roof was at least five feet lower than this one on which he stood. He paused for only a moment, took a couple of backward steps, then ran forward, leaping out into space. He dropped on to his heels, steadied himself and then ran on, hurrying now. Another leap and he was on the roof of the sheriff's office. As he had hoped, there was a wide drainpipe running down the rear wall. Shinning down it, he landed softly in the yard at the back.

A faint glimmer of light showed through the small square window set in the back of the building. Trying the door, he found it locked but the window opened as he slid the blade of the knife under the rotting wood and prised it loose. The light, he discovered, came along the short passage running between the two rows of iron-barred cells. The door at the far end stood open and he judged that Kerdy was now in the outer office. This view received confirmation as he edged softly forward and picked out the low murmur of voices.

Approaching the half-open door, he pressed his ear to it, listening intently. Kerdy was there, but he did not recognize the other voice.

'You got any idea why this hombre

came back to Mendaro, Kerdy?'

'Hell! Ain't it obvious? He must've heard about that pard of his.'

'You mean Dave Lawson?'

'Who else? Could be he's figurin' on evenin' the score. Goin' up against Mendoza.'

'Reckon that'd suit your book. Mendoza and his men will have him up in Boot Hill before the night's out.'

'They'd better. I don't like the idea of that hellion runnin' around loose in the night yonder. The sooner he's brought back here with a bullet in him, the better I'll feel.'

There came a faint chuckle, then the unknown man said: 'Better lock this door when I leave, Kerdy. He might decide to make a try for you while the Vigilantes are out lookin' for him.'

A moment later, there was the sound of the street door opening and closing and then, quite distinctly, the turning of a heavy key in the lock. He heard Kerdy move back into the room followed by the creak of a chair. Waiting no longer, he threw open the door and stepped through, standing with his legs braced.

Behind the long mahogany desk, Kerdy suddenly twisted around in his chair eyes popping from his head, his face blanched. He half rose to his feet, then fell back as Brad moved forward purposefully. One stride took him to the edge of the desk. Leaning forward, he grabbed the other by the shirt, pulling him halfway over the desk.

'So you were in on the killin' of Dave Lawson,' he gritted harshly. There was cold menace in his tone. Kerdy recognized it and the expression of fear increased.

'I knew nothin' of it until I walked into Forlan's office and found Lawson there with a gun on Jess. I'd have locked him up in the jail here and given him a chance to cool off before orderin' him to ride out of town and stay out, only he forced us both at gunpoint across to the saloon where he called out Mendoza. Weren't nothin' I could do about that.'

'You could've brought Mendoza in for trial.'

The other shook his head, his flabby cheeks mottled. 'You serious? I'd have stood even less chance of pullin' that off than Lawson did. At least he had his gun in his hand when he made his play.'

'And you're tellin' me that even with that advantage he didn't have a chance against Mendoza?'

'Hell! I'm only tellin' you exactly what happened.'

'And I'm tellin' you to your face that you're a goddamn liar, Kerdy! I heard you send those so-called Vigilantes of yours out after me.'

'I — ' The other swallowed thickly, then fell back heavily in the chair as Brad thrust him away.

'Now you're just goin' to sit tight there and answer a few questions. If I get what seem to be the right answers I might think twice about lettin' you keep your miserable hide.'

'I don't know a damn thing,' grunted the other. His eyes darted around the room like those of a trapped animal.

'No? Let's start with Forlan. Just where does he fit in to all this? What's his connection with Mendoza?'

'What's that got to do with me? I just try to keep law and order in town. If Forlan is in cahoots with Mendoza then he sure keeps it to himself.'

Brad slipped one of the long-bladed throwing knives from his belt, turned it over and over in his hands so that the light from the desk lamp, reflected off the glittering blade, flashed in the other's eyes. Kerdy watched it as though mesmerised. He lay quite still with his mouth hanging slackly open, breathing heavily.

'Reckon I'll have to jog your memory a little.' Brad leaned forward until the tip of the blade touched the other's neck just under the chin. He exerted a slight pressure and a tiny drop of blood appeared where the cold steel penetrated the flesh. Sweat beaded the lawman's forehead and began to trickle down the folds of his skin.

Brad grinned. 'You still aim to keep your mouth buttoned tight?'

Kerdy lifted a shaking hand towards the knife, then drew it away with a sharp motion. 'All right,' he croaked, 'so there's some tie-in between 'em. But that's all I know, so help me. Now take that damn knife away from my throat.'

'Not yet. You know Mendoza's men by sight?'

'Most of 'em, why?' The other ran the tip of his tongue around his lips.

'Callaghan's herd was rustled last night by some hombres who looked like part of his bunch. Was Mendoza and all of his crew in town last night?'

'Far as I know.'

Judging from the way the other was shaking, Brad reckoned that he was telling the truth. Easing himself back, he withdrew the knife. Gradually, some of the fear faded from the sheriff's face, to be replaced by a growing look of confidence. He heaved his ponderous bulk up in the chair.

'Now that I've told you all this, just

what do you intend doin' with the information? You can't get out of Mendaro, that much is for sure. Every road out will be watched by armed men. They'll all shoot on sight and they all know what the price of failure is. Either they get you, or Forlan gets them. Not much of a choice, is it?'

Brad's lip curled. 'I can always use you as a shield, Kerdy. With that bulk, you could stop a dozen bullets before they get one through to me.'

'You'd never get away with it. They wouldn't hesitate to shoot just because I was there. Forlan has too much at stake and he knows I'm not indispensable.'

Brad deliberated that remark. There was undoubtedly some truth in what the other said. If Forlan was all that folk made him out to be, Kerdy's death would mean little or nothing to him.

'Get on your feet, Kerdy,' he said abruptly. 'I'm takin' you back to the Flying Y. I figure that Callaghan might want to hear some of what you've just told me and — '

He broke off abruptly as a loud tap sounded on the street door. A voice yelled out: 'You still in there, Sheriff?'

'Just keep your mouth shut if you want to stay alive,' Brad hissed softly. He brought the Colt out from its holster in a blur of motion, trained it on the lawman's head. Kerdy shrank back into the chair, licking his lips.

There was a momentary pause, then a second voice from just outside the door said harshly: 'Somethin's wrong, Reston. Kerdy wouldn't leave without puttin' out the light.'

Something hard hammered at the locked door. Moving swiftly around the desk, Brad brought the barrel of the Colt down hard on the sheriff's head as the other made to lunge to his feet. The man collapsed without a moan. Seconds later, the window crashed into the room and Brad saw the pale blur of a man's face in the opening, caught the glimpse of lamplight glinting off a metal barrel. Brad dropped to his knees instantly, heard the slam of the bullet in the desk a split second after the report of the Colt. The pearl-handled Colt seemed to leap into his fist as if it had a life all its own. His first shot smashed the lamp on the desk, sending oil spilling all over the polished wood; the second shot the remaining glass from the window. In the darkness he heard a loud yell go up as the lead found its mark and he saw a dim shape leap and then fall away into the street.

This was no time for him to be waiting around, he decided. Turning, still in a crouch, he made for the rear door, knocking his shins against a chair. Heavy blows sounded on the locked door of the office and he heard the splintering of wood. From outside, there came a chorus of shouts as more men were called to the scene.

Slamming the connecting door behind him, he raced along the narrow corridor, reached the back door and opened it, peering out into the night. The sound of running feet in the nearby alley came echoing out of the dimness. It sounded as though half a dozen men or more were racing around to the back to cut him off while the others burst in at the front.

Thrusting the Colt back into leather, he ran for the high fence some ten yards away, jumped and gripped the top with both hands, throwing himself over it. He landed on his side, lay for a moment with all of the wind knocked out of him. More shouting reached his ears as he lay on the hard sun-baked earth.

'You men spread out,' roared a loud voice. 'Benson and Chivers, you come with me into the jail. If he's still in there, we've got him covered.'

Getting quietly to his feet, Brad moved away into the night. He had gone less than fifteen yards when a couple of shots rang out behind him. An invisible hand seemed to pluck at his sleeve.

'That's him!' shouted a man harshly. 'Over yonder!'

Without pausing to look around, knowing that he would have the pack of them on his neck within seconds, Brad raced forward into the concealing shadows. Slugs hummed viciously through the air all about him as he bobbed and weaved from side to side to present a more difficult target to the gunmen. Risking a quick look over his shoulder as he ran, he spotted them moving around the end of the fence, the man in the lead signalling to the others to spread out on either side of him, to circle around and cut him off. Gritting his teeth, he continued to run, eyes searching for a place where he might throw his pursuers off. These men knew this town far better than he did, knew all of the short cuts among the low-roofed buildings which lay in front of him.

In front of him the ground sloped downward steeply, littered with boulders and clods of overturned earth. Feet slipping on the treacherous ground, Brad ran into a narrow culvert, the earthen walls rising above shoulder level. He knew the men would expect him to keep on to the end and halfway along it, he stopped, gripped the crumbling wall to his left and hauled himself up into the tangle of brush which lined it. Throwing himself sideways, he lay quite still with the sharp thorns pressing into his flesh.

He heard them come on, slackening their pace a little, wary now in case he might be lying in wait for them. They outnumbered him by a dozen to one, but they knew that he could take two or three of them with him and there was not a single man among them who wanted to be in that number.

Keeping his body absolutely still, moving only his eyes, he made out the dim shapes, saw them hesitate as they came to the culvert. Then two of them moved into it with drawn guns, their faces vague blurs. They drew level with his hiding place, walking slowly and warily, then went on by, passing so close that he could have reached out a hand and touched them.

'He in there?' shouted one of the men.

'Nope. Must've gone on.' The voice came from the distant end of the opening.

'Damn! Still, he can't get far. The rest of the boys will have swung around the stores. They'll cut him off before long. He must've left his mount somewhere in town and he won't try to cross the desert on foot. Be a damn fool if he does.'

'He might be hidin' out in one of these buildings,' suggested another man. 'If he is, he can pick some of us off the minute we show ourselves.'

'We'll get him, even if we have to keep the whole place surrounded until daylight,' muttered the other. There was the scrape of a match and a brief orange flare picked out the other's features under the brim of the hat. Lying there, Brad recognised the gunhawk as Reston. Flicking the spent match away, the two men remained standing at the entrance to the culvert for several moments, then moved off after the others.

He waited until the sound of pursuit had died away into the distance and the faint yells of the searching men could only just be picked out from the multitude of other night sounds, then got to his feet and moved stealthily back in the direction of the town, cutting around the outskirts so as to wind up near the eastern end of the main street.

Most of the activity was now centred on the far side of Mendaro and there were few people visible along the entire length of the street. Stepping up on to the boardwalk, he threaded his way along it, moving on to where he had left Big Jet. Apart from what he had learned from Kerdy, his night here had been all but wasted and he had almost got himself killed in the process. It was small wonder that Lawson hadn't stood a chance coming here on a mission of revenge.

Stepping into the alley which led out

towards the grain stores, he increased his pace. A couple of shots sounded from the far end of town and he guessed that the men hunting him were getting a mite jumpy and shooting at shadows. But it would not be long before they cast their net wider in the hope of trapping him. Even now, he doubted if they would have been foolish enough to pull in those men ordered to watch the trails out of town and he could expect trouble before he got clear.

It was this realization which saved him a little while later. As he moved around the edge of one of the long wooden buildings, he caught the sudden movement directly ahead of him. Cursing, he checked his stride and pulled back under the cover of a narrow doorway.

There were three men less than twenty yards away standing in a loose bunch around Big Jet. Bitterly, he berated himself for not having considered the possibility that some of the gunhawks might come across his mount. One of the men tried to pull the reins free of the rail, jumped back smartly as the black stallion lashed out with a hind leg. Brad thinned his lips as he drew his Colt. He saw the man circle round again, approach Big Jet from the side. Jerking out his hand, he succeeded in loosening the reins. For a moment, the animal remained quiet, then Brad stepped out into the open stretch of ground and gave a low-pitched whistle. In the same instant that the three gunslingers whirled to face him, grabbing for their weapons, Big Jet reared up in answer to the signal. One of the men suddenly went down in a crumpled heap and lay still in the dust.

The others began firing at the tall shape facing them, moving apart to take him from two sides. A slug ricocheted off an upjutting rock near Brad's feet and tore a long sliver of wood from the wall of the building. Then the Colt jerked twice against his wrist. Brad's face was grim, promising no mercy for the killers. In the sharp bloom of gun-fire, he saw the nearer man stagger, fold at the knees and pitch forward beside his fallen companion, his gun falling from fingers no longer having the strength to hold it. The third man came on in a blundering rush, still firing. But he was swaying on his feet like a drunken man with lead somewhere deep within him, only a savage anger keeping him upright as the life drained swiftly out of him with the blood that stained the front of his checked shirt.

Two slugs bounced off the ground in front of him as the gun barrel tilted inevitably downward. Lunging to one side, he flung out an arm, clawed at the post beside him. For several seconds he remained hanging there struggling desperately to bring up the gun for one last shot at the tall man before him. Then his legs gave under him and he slid down the post into an ungainly heap, his hat crushing into the dust as his head went down. His legs gave a final spasmodic twitch and then he lay still.

Going forward, keeping the Colt trained on them, Brad bent briefly to examine their bodies. All three were dead and, swinging up into the saddle, aware of the necessity of getting out of Mendaro as quickly as possible before the shooting attracted attention, he put Big Jet through a narrow alley, found himself in more open ground, and gave the stallion its head.

He allowed his horse to travel at its own pace until he was well clear of town, then eased up its headlong rush with a slight pull on the reins. By now, he was out in the trackless desert which lay to the north-west of Mendaro and, having ridden over several long stretches of bare rock, doubted if any of the men behind him would be able to follow his trail.

By midnight, he was in tall timber country where rolling foothills bordered the mountains still several miles in the distance but dominating the night skyline. There was bright starlight, sufficient to give him plenty of light to see by and, edging up into the hills, he picked himself a spot well away from the bare rock and made cold camp.

Stretching out on his blanket, he lay for a long while, listening to the night sounds all about him, the furtive rustlings in the undergrowth around the tall trees. Then, rolling over on to his side, he closed his eyes and slept.

When he woke, it was just getting light. The last of the sky sentinels was fading over to the west and there was a brightening greyness along the rim of the eastern horizon and a faint, rosy flush touching the crests of the mountains. Big Jet stood patiently a few yards away. Getting to his feet, he stretched his stiff limbs, drank his fill from a small, swift-flowing stream nearby, then moved towards the outer fringe of the trees, surveying the terrain across which he had ridden a few hours earlier.

Rolling himself a smoke, he took in everything in an all-embracing glance, then stiffened abruptly as he spotted the dust cloud off in the direction of Mendaro. He judged that the riders were perhaps three or four miles away, but their track would bring them closer to this part of the foothills, maybe too close for comfort. He recalled that some of the Mexicans working with Forlan might be sufficiently good trackers to follow his trail even across bare rock.

Eyes narrowed down, he watched the men come on. They must have been hitting the trail all night for their mounts seemed tired and the men were strung out at wide intervals. Seeing this, he thinned his lips down as an idea came to him. Maybe he would be able to pick off a prisoner for himself after all.

Sliding back into the trees, he found the narrow game track which angled off to his left and followed it for a hundred yards to the point where it ran along the rim of a deep canyon cut in the bare rock. He had already judged that if those men decided to come up into the hills after him, they would choose this path which offered them the least resistance to the thick timber further to his right.

Settling himself down in a cleft in the rocks, he uncoiled the lariat from his belt, slid the smooth hemp through his fingers. A swarm of tiny heel flies settled over his head, their vicious bites stinging his flesh as he waited with a stony patience. The sound of the approaching horses grew louder in his ears and he could pick out the curses of the men as they pushed their weary mounts up through the boulders. Keeping his head down, he scanned the narrow trail where it led up from the lower reaches. Two minutes later, he spotted the first of the men, recognised Reston with Crawley close behind him. Brad's hands tightened around the rope. The men came on at a slow pace, their eyes flicking nervously from side to side, one of them bending low in the saddle to scan the ground underfoot, looking for tracks.

Reston suddenly reined up his mount, pulled in to the side, waving the rest of the riders on. Pressing his body hard against the rock, Brad heard the men move by, angling higher along the trail, up to where the pines stood tall against the dawn sky. They passed around the sharp bend in the canyon out of sight and there was only Reston left, sitting tall in the saddle, peering about him with suspicious eyes. Then the other touched spurs to his mount, gigging it on towards the spot where Brad lay in wait.

Brad let him go by, then eased himself up, spun the lariat outward. It swung high; the noose opening, dropping over the man's unsuspecting shoulders. With a swift jerk of his wrists, he pulled the noose tight, jerking Reston out of the saddle. The gunhawk hit the rocky ground hard, rolled over limply as his head struck an outcrop of sandstone. He was still conscious but too dazed to make any cry of alarm and, running forward, Brad struck him on the head with the butt of the Colt.

Swiftly, knowing that the other would soon be missed, he dragged the unconscious man up into the boulders, hauled him behind the protective safety of a giant tree stump. The man's horse stood at the end of the canyon, trembling. Leaving Reston, Brad leapt down, jumped for the swinging bridle and swung the horse around, slapping it hard across the rump, sending it racing back along the way it had come. The sound of the retreating riders suddenly ceased in the distance and he knew that they were probably wondering what had become of Reston. Racing back into the rocks, he came up to the fallen gunslinger, bent and pulled him across his shoulders.

As he gained the comparative sanctuary of the trees, he glanced back, saw the men struggling along the trail, evidently searching for their comrade. He saw one of them suddenly lift a hand and pointed off towards the desert where a small dust cloud marked the position of the runaway horse. He did not wait any longer to see whether they would pull out after the running mount or begin searching the rocks.

Reaching the spot where he had made camp, he slung the unconscious man over the saddle, then swung up behind him, his face grim as he rode down the slope. There was an icy glint in his eyes which betokened his attitude to what was going on around Mendaro. Reaching the edge of the foothills where they sloped westward down in the direction of the Flying Y spread, he scanned the terrain behind him, but there was no sign of his pursuers. Either they had gone after that riderless mount, or they were still busy scouring the timber for some sign of him and Reston.

Touching spurs to Big Jet's flanks, he urged the stallion forward at a quick trot, wanting to put as much distance as possible between himself and the gunhawks who were after his blood. It would not be long, he knew, before they came after him.

5

Guns of Fury

The stunted trees, the harsh glare of the alkali and the huge, sky-rearing buttes, their bases levelled in the shifted dust, grew less hostile as he approached the southern edge of the Flying Y spread. Riding in through the gate, he made his way to the line camp where he found Flint and several of the crew eating a late breakfast. They eyed the limp figure over the pommel in some surprise as Brad slid from the saddle, then the foreman got to his feet and walked over.

'Who's this hombre Brad?'

'He goes by the handle of Reston. I ran into him last night with a few of his friends. They trailed me out from the hills. I managed to jump this one. I reckon that maybe he'll talk once I get him to Callaghan.'

Flint grinned wolfishly. 'If he's one of them gunhawks, I guess we can make him talk right here. Just what it is you want him to tell?'

'I'd like to know if he was with that bunch who rustled the steers the other night. If he was, then he can tell us where they are and any plans those outlaws may have for the future.' Brad walked over to the fire as he spoke, hunkered down on his heels and gratefully accepted the mug of hot coffee that was handed to him.

'Anythin' else?'

'Maybe he can tell us who's behind all this thievin' and killin'.'

The other shrugged. 'Ain't that obvious. It's Forlan. He's the only one who really stands to gain from this. There's talk goin' around that he's buyin' up those other spreads as soon as the folk are either forced out or shot down in cold blood.'

Brad finished the coffee, brow knit in concentration. 'I guess it does look that way. But there are some things that puzzle me, some loose ends that are hangin' around and nothin' to tie 'em on to.'

'Hell! I'd have said it was a cut and dried case against him. We know that he must be in cahoots with Mendoza, otherwise he could never have guaranteed to stop those bandits hittin' the men who paid him protection money.'

'Seems to me that's what everybody thinks. Somehow, I'm beginnin' to doubt it, although there ain't a thing that can prove I'm right.'

Flint thrust his thumbs into his belt, legs straddled. There was a tight look of speculation on his bluff features. 'Let's start by bringin' this killer round and gettin' somethin' out of him,' he suggested. 'You've set me thinkin' too now.'

Without waiting for Brad to get to his feet, the foreman went over to the fire and picked up a pail of water standing there. Going across to where Reston lay stretched out on the grass, he flung the contents over the unconscious man's face. Reston jerked slightly, then coughed as the ice-cold water went into his throat, threatening to choke him. With a muttered oath, he pushed himself into a sitting position, blinking his eyes and staring about him.

When he saw the men standing around him, his right hand flashed down towards his gunbelt, encountered the empty holster. With the realization that he was a prisoner, an expression of truculent anger spread over his face.

'What's the meanin' of this?' he snapped. 'Who the hell are you?'

Flint grinned down at him but there was nothing pleasant about his smile. 'We're the Flying Y crew,' he said quietly. 'You got anythin' to say before we start draggin' it out of you the hard way?'

The other did not answer but twisted his head, staring across the fire at Brad. The look of hate in his eyes was plain for them all to see.

'Let me ask him, Flint.' Kernahan came forward, holding a leather quirt in his hands. 'Anythin' you want to know, I'll make him tell you.'

'Keep your shirt on,' said Flint harshly. 'We'll see if he's got any sense first. You can always use that if he decides to stay stubborn.'

'You whip me and I'll see all of you in hell,' grated the other.

'You'll sure go there first,' Flint told him, 'unless you open your mouth and answer our questions.'

'There's not a damn thing I can tell you.'

'No? Reckon you ain't heard that our herd was rustled a couple of nights ago. Five hundred head driven off and three men dead.'

'What's that got to do with me? I know nothin' about it.'

'And I'm allowin' that you do.' Brad spoke evenly as he came forward and stood over the other. 'You're in thick with Mendoza and his murderin' band. You know everythin' that goes on.'

'I'm waitin',' said Flint ominously. He gave a meaningful glance at the quirt in Kernahan's hands. 'If I have to turn this fella on you to make you talk, he'll take all of the flesh off your back in little strips and you'll tell us what we want to know anyway. So why not save yourself all that trouble?'

Reston ran his tongue around lips that were suddenly dry. He hunched his shoulders back and looked distinctly uncomfortable. One look at the faces of the men surrounding him told him that they meant every word, that they had done with ordinary methods and had now been pushed to the limit.

'All right, so I've ridden with Mendoza,' he said monotonously, eyes flicking from one man to another. 'But I weren't with that bunch who raided the herd.'

'But they were Mendoza's men?'

Reston gave a quick nod. 'Mendoza stayed in town with the others. Sent twenty or so men out here. They had orders to jump you at this camp and drive off as many steers as they could.'

'And Mendoza? Who does he take his

orders from? There's somebody big at the back of him, giving the commands.'

'Why should he take orders from anybody? He's big enough to give any orders himself.'

'And what about the cattle,' asked Brad flatly. 'Across the border?'

'Far as I know, that was the plan. You don't have a chance of gettin' any of 'em back, so you might as well forget it.'

Brad shook his head decisively. 'That ain't the way I see it. Sure he could get a fair price for beef across the border, but he's not in the rustlin' business for that.'

'If there is anybody at the back of him, I reckon you'd best ask Mendoza yourself.' There was naked scorn in the other's tone now as he looked Brad up and down. 'If you've got the guts to do it, that is.'

'There'll come a time and a place for that,' Brad promised evenly. He turned to Flint. 'You got any place here where you can lock this killer up for the night?

I'll ride in and let Callaghan know what's happened. He might want to do things his way.' He shot a quick look down at the prisoner. 'Might be he'll decide to string you up along the trail someplace as a warnin' to the rest of your breed.'

'I'll find a place for him,' the foreman promised. 'If he tries to make a break for it, he'll collect a bullet for his pains.'

Two of the crew caught Reston by the arms and hustled him off into one of the cabins. Brad knew that they would be as good as their word. They had seen three of their companions killed by Mendoza's men and he knew that none of them was likely to forget it. Reston was in good hands.

Before going to his mount, he said quietly to the foreman: 'Best post a couple of men as lookouts. The rest of that band might decide to cut their trail in this direction, especially if they've figured out now what happened to him. They may want to get him back, or put a slug into him to stop him tellin' too much.'

'We'll be ready for 'em,' gritted the other grimly.

* * *

The glare of the sun was terrific as Brad headed into it around high noon. This southern edge of the Flying Y spread was made up of coarse grass and chaparral, interspersed with clumps of sharp-edge Spanish Sword, and he deliberately skirted around it, not wanting to risk Big Jet in the fearsome underbrush where a horse's feet could be slashed to ribbons in minutes. Ahead of him lay undulating country, bordered far to the south by a line of upthrusting sandstone buttes which formed the boundary of the spread in that direction.

Heat lay like a smothering blanket all about him and, wiping the sweat from his face, he urged Big Jet about the high rocky face and found himself staring off into a wide valley, hidden almost completely from view in other directions by the tall walls of sandstone which all but surrounded it. Staring down the long, narrow slope, he made out the small herd of cattle clustered together in the centre of the valley and the small camp off to one side. Brow knit in puzzlement, he let his glance roam over the scene.

This was, as far as he knew, Flying Y land, yet he had heard nothing of any part of the herd being bedded down here, miles away from the main part of the stock. A little nagging suspicion rose in his mind as he watched the men around the camp. Even from that distance, it was possible to see that they were not dressed like normal cowhands.

Alert and stiffly tensed in the saddle, he sat motionless. It seemed incredible, but from what he could see, those cattle down there were the five hundred head or so which had been rustled a few nights before. Yet why had these men brought them here instead of driving them clear across the Mexico border? Their actions just didn't seem to make any sense at all. Turning Big Jet, he picked his way carefully along the rock face, found a track which led downward in the direction of the herd and moved cautiously along it, his thoughts spinning chaotically in his head. There had to be an answer to it somewhere, he figured. But at the moment he could think of none. Unless those men down there were waiting for the main outlaw force to ride out from Mendaro and help them with the drive into Mexico.

For several moments, the tall pinnacles of sandstone cut off all view of the valley and when he came out into an open spot again, he saw that he was now less than half a mile from the small knot of men. There was now no doubt in his mind as to their identity. Loosening the Colt in its holster, he checked the chambers, thrust a fresh shell in from his belt, then swung down from the saddle. He moved swiftly, noiselessly, seeking out the grassy patches of ground, his feet making no noise.

Slackening his pace as he neared the camp, fearful lest he dislodge any of the flat pieces of shale which abounded in this region, he came up behind an outcrop of stone which provided him with ample cover from where he could watch the activity below him without fear of discovery.

There were six men down there, entirely oblivious of his presence, their mounts staked out some distance from the camp itself. Most of the men were seated around a fire, their backs to him. One man lay under blankets a couple of yards away, but it was impossible to tell if he were asleep or had been wounded. Then, one of the other outlaws pushed himself to his feet, went across to the blanketed figure and lifted the man's head, holding a mug to his lips. Brad eyed the men appraisingly. They all wore holsters strapped securely to their thighs, a sign of a gunman, such strapped-down holsters facilitating a rapid draw. He nodded grimly to himself, debating his next move. As far as he could see there were no other men with the herd and the number of horses tallied with the men. Either he stepped out into the open and threw down on them, or he left as silently as he had come, getting word through to Callaghan, bringing back more men to round up these killers and the herd.

He had never been a man to back away from a showdown, but prudence warned him that with six men he would be risking his neck for nothing. He could take one or two of them with him, but if he was killed, then no one would be any the wiser of what had happened. Gently, he slid back around the rocks, moved along the upgrade to where he had left Big Jet. Judging from the camp down there, these men were in no particular hurry to get up and leave and the fact that they must have hidden out here for more than a day since driving off those cattle, indicated that he had little to lose riding back to the Flying Y ranch and warning Callaghan.

Stepping up into the saddle, he headed north, cutting across the white alkali towards the distant ranch. Overhead, the sun commenced its westward slide towards the horizon and gradually, there came a welcome coolness to the air as evening came on. By the time he sighted the ranch, it was almost dark and there were yellow lights showing in the windows as he entered the wide courtyard and slid from the saddle on the run.

Callaghan was near the corral fence, came over to him, flicking away a cigarette. 'Figured you was finished for sure,' he said by way of greeting. 'I was on the point of gettin' some of the boys together and ridin' into town to see what had transpired.'

'I'm all right,' Brad said tightly. 'But I've found those five hundred head you lost a couple of nights back.'

He saw the sudden gust of expression that flicked over the rancher's face, then it was gone and the other said harshly: 'The hell you have. Where are they?'

'About twenty miles south of here. This side of the border, down near the Badlands.'

Callaghan whistled thinly through his teeth. 'I could have sworn they'd be clear into Mexico by now. You sure they're Flying Y stock?'

'Pretty certain. Naturally, I couldn't get too close to 'em to make out the brand. But there were six hombres campin' there and they sure looked like those men who hit us on the range that night. Besides, they're still on your land.'

'You feel like ridin' out again tonight?' demanded the other harshly, eyeing him up and down.

'Sure thing.'

'Then get yourself a bite to eat at the cookhouse and I'll be ready in fifteen minutes. This I've got to see for myself.'

★ ★ ★

Jeb Callaghan was already mounted up by the corral fence when Brad came back after eating a hasty meal. As he swung up into the saddle, he stared about him in surprise. 'Ain't you takin' any of the men with you?' he inquired, puzzled.

The rancher shook his head. 'We can get all the men we need from the line camp after we've looked this place over. From what you say, those critters didn't look like for pullin' out in a hurry and if we was to ride up on them in a big bunch they'd pick up the sound of our horses miles away and be drivin' those steers clear across the border before we got a smell of 'em. This is the best way. I want to check just who they are and that those are my cattle before we rush in at half-cock.'

Brad shrugged. It was the other's play. If he wanted it this way, it was all right with him, though at the moment it just didn't seem to make sense.

They rode out of the courtyard in the growing darkness and cut south, riding in silence, each man engrossed in his own private thoughts. They rode quickly, wasting no time, with Brad slightly in the lead, cutting through gullies and across grassy plains, heading for the point where the Badlands began.

An hour's hard riding brought them in sight of the tall buttes which Brad had noticed early that afternoon. He reined up, pointed a hand in their direction. 'That's where they was holed up,' he said softly.

Callaghan rubbed a hand over his chin thoughtfully. 'Big Mesa valley,' he grunted. 'Seems a logical place for them to hide out. Ain't often anyone goes there. Only thing that puzzles me is why they didn't keep on goin' after they'd run 'em off.'

'I've been wonderin' about that myself,' Brad commented. 'Could be that they're waitin' for Mendoza to ride out from town. They must know this country like the backs of their hands to pull a brazen stunt like this.'

'It sure looks that way,' agreed the

other after a pause. 'Let's go take a look-see. If they're still there we'll bring up the boys from the camp and give those coyotes a lesson they'll never forget.'

Edging their mounts on at a slow trot, they entered the area of rock which overlooked the valley, stepping out of the saddle once they gained the shelter of the tumbled boulders. As he made to move forward, Callaghan caught his arm, whispered: 'We'll split up here. They may have posted look-outs now that it's dark. We'll stand a better chance that way of slippin' through. You say there was six of 'em when you spotted their camp?'

'That's right, though one looked as if he had been hurt bad.'

'That leaves only five to take care of if they do spot us.' Callaghan considered that for a moment, then inclined his head off to the right. 'I'll take this way. You go that. We'll meet back here unless anythin' happens.'

He slid away into the enshrouding

darkness and a moment later, as the soft pad of his feet on the rocks died away, Brad edged off to his left, squeezing himself between two upthrusting boulders. He moved on for twenty yards or so, then halted and listened intently for any sound. The stillness of the night lay all about him and there was not even the tell-tale lowing of the cattle to break the silence. Puzzled, he went on, lowering himself down a steep, shale-littered slope, picking his way with extra care, feeling for footholds before trusting himself to put all of his weight down. It would be so easy to slip here, to send a shower of stones down that uneven slope and alert those outlaws.

On the eastern horizon, a pale yellow glow heralded the rising moon. Soon it would flood the entire valley, making everything almost as bright as day.

There was a movement of some sort directly ahead of him and he pressed himself hard against the rock, blending in with the shadows. Quietly, he eased the Colt out of its holster, held it tightly in his fist, his finger on the trigger. There came the soft, furtive scrape of cloth against rock as the man came on. Now, he was able to pick out the faint shape, just visible against the skyline. So these men had posted look-outs! Thinning his lips back across his teeth, he wormed his way around the rear of the rock to bring himself behind the man and at a slightly higher level. The man was there all right, clearly visible now, his back to him.

Even as he watched, the other shifted his position slightly, felt inside his jacket pocket, brought out a cheroot and thrust it between his lips. The flare of the match had scarcely died before Brad moved. Sliding around the rock, he rammed the barrel of the Colt hard into the other's back, hissed:

'One sound out of you, *amigo*, and it'll be your last.'

The sentry stiffened, but did not turn his head. Reaching down with his free hand, Brad jerked the weapons from the other's belt, let them drop into the dust. There was a curious eagerness about him now which he found impossible to explain.

'All right,' he said softly. 'Now turn around and let's have a look at you.'

He took a step back as the other obeyed, then spun quickly as another sound came from almost directly behind him. He caught a fragmentary glimpse of a second figure less than ten feet away, raised his gun. Before he could pull the trigger, orange-blue flame lashed through the darkness, a blinding flash that was accompanied by a thunderous roar which beat momentarily at his ears. Something like a white-hot branding iron seared at his face, seemed to burn deep in his flesh. There came a hammer blow at the side of his head and he staggered back, the Colt slipping from his nerveless fingers. Dimly, he was aware of the dark shape moving purposefully towards him out of a darkness which seemed to be growing blacker with every fleeting second. All of his strength seemed to be flowing from his body and there was suddenly no feeling in his arms and legs.

Frantically, he tried to stay on his feet, fighting doggedly against the blackness which came out of the rocks to engulf him, knowing that if he once let himself slip into it, he might never come out of it again. For what seemed an eternity, he lay slumped against the side of the rock face, striving to draw air into his aching chest. His head seemed to have become swollen to twice its normal size and there was a pounding inside his brain as though something in there was desperately trying to burst out.

Then the darkness rose up from the ground, drawing him down into it, irresistible and overpowering. His head slumped forward and his legs buckled, pitching him on to his face in the cold dust.

★　★　★

Brad's first awareness was of bitter cold and a numbness which seemed to hold his body in an iron grip, refusing to release its hold on his limbs. He tried to move his arms but they were as lead weights, without any life of their own. With a conscious effort, he forced his eyes open. Darkness lay all about him, thick and absolute, with nothing moving in it. He drew in a shuddering breath and only the fact that he heard a wheezing in through his open mouth told him that he was still alive.

For several minutes, he lay quite still and gradually some of the feeling came back into his limbs. Flexing his fingers, he forced them to move, then managed to raise his right arm a little way, feeling the side of his head. There was a crusty dryness on his temple and the hammering started up again whenever he moved.

The moon had lifted into the clear sky and he judged that he had been out for some time. Carefully, he looked around him. There was no sign of the men who had attacked him nor of Callaghan. The thought of the other sent a stab of urgency through him. Where was Jeb? Had he been jumped too? Was he lying dead somewhere out there among the rocks? He knew that he had to move now, whether he felt like it or not. Placing the palms of his hands against the hard ground, he levered himself up on to his knees, knelt there for a moment while the agony in his skull lessened, then pulled himself to his feet, holding on to the rock for support. As he moved his foot struck something metallic and bending, he found it was the Colt, which lay where it had fallen.

Thrusting it back into his holster, he felt a trifle easier in his mind. At least, he was not unarmed and if those men did come back, he could still give a good account of himself in spite of the head wound. Gingerly, aware of the weakness in him, he moved around the huge boulder, was on the point of tackling the steep upgrade, when a dark figure came down from the higher levels. His right hand dropped towards the Colt, then he stayed the movement as a familiar voice said:

'Hold it, Brad. It's me — Callaghan.'

The rancher came down to him, caught his arm. 'Hell! I thought you'd be out for the rest of the night. I just left you five minutes ago and you were still out cold. I went to look for some water to clean up that head of yours.'

Weakly, Brad sank down against the rock as the other poured water from his canteen on to his kerchief. The ice-cold liquid stung his flesh as the other began to clean away the dried blood on his temple and he gritted his teeth as lances of agony burned their way clear through his skull.

'You any idea what happened?' asked the other after a little while. 'I heard the shot and came hot-footin' it over, but by the time I got here the coyote who had done the shootin' had skedaddled.'

Brad reached for the canteen which the other held out and gulped down some of the water before replying. 'I came on this hombre in the rocks, grabbed his guns. But there was another of 'em. I reckon he must've fired that shot. I don't seem to remember much about it.'

'You were damned lucky. From that distance, I don't see how the hell he could've missed. There are powder burns on your face so he couldn't have been more than a couple of feet away. Guess they must've figured you for dead and pulled out in case there were any more of us around.'

'What about the herd? They still around?'

The other hesitated a moment, then shook his head, pushing the cork back into the canteen. 'There was no herd,' he said thinly. 'I've been over most of that valley down there and can find neither hide nor hair of 'em.'

Brad pressed his lips together into a tight line as he detected the faint note of disbelief in the rancher's tone. 'They were there all right this afternoon,' he asserted harshly.

'They sure aren't there now. Without any of those cattle, I'd never be able to prove they were mine.'

Brad shook his head in an attempt to clear it, winced as a further flash of pain stabbed through him. The wound had begun to bleed again, but gradually, his mind was clearing. Lurching upright, he followed the other down the slope, out into the moonlit valley. The chilly night air brought some of the life back into him and he felt the strength beginning to return.

Carefully, they made a search of the valley. The remains of a campfire were where Brad had seen the outlaws earlier but the grey ashes had been covered with dirt and were quite cold. In places, too, they found where the tough, wiry grass had been grazed and there were marks where the cattle had been.

Callaghan came over from examining a low ridge, his face grim. 'We'll find nothin' here that we could possibly use as evidence,' he said sourly. 'Better ride into the line camp and report this to Flint and the others. We'd also better have a look at that head wound. You lost quite a heap of blood back there.'

'I'll make out.' Brad spoke more sharply than he had intended. There was something here which didn't quite add up and the thought continued to trouble him as they made their way back to the horses. That man who had fired at him, cutting him down — why hadn't he made sure he was dead before leaving? It was possible that Callaghan was right and the two rustlers had pulled out in case there were any more men lurking around in the shadows, but it would have been the work of only a moment to have put another bullet into him and made certain that he didn't live.

There was little activity at the line camp when they rode in at just after two o'clock in the morning. A couple of men stepped out of the shadows of one of the buildings, Winchesters covering them. Then Flint came forward.

'Somethin' wrong, boss?' he asked, staring up at Callaghan.

The rancher jerked a thumb at Brad. 'Lando here spotted a herd in Big Mesa valley this afternoon, came and reported to me. He figured they were part of the herd rustled the other night so we rode out for a look-see.'

'Find anythin'?'

'We ran into some trouble with a couple of hombres there, but no sign of the cattle. They must've run 'em out some time durin' the afternoon. Brad stopped a slug for his pains.'

The big foreman turned his glance on the other as Brad stepped down. 'I'll get Ephraim to take a look at it. He knows somethin' of doctorin'.'

Turning, he yelled for the other and a moment later, Ephraim came out of the building, pulling on his jacket. While the other tended to the head wound, Callaghan and Flint drew off some distance and conversed together in low tones.

'You catch any sight of the man who

shot you?' Ephraim asked as he tied the bandage.

Brad shook his head. 'He stayed in the shadows whoever he was. But I'd know the other coyote if I ever see him again.'

'Must've been a couple of men they left behind in case Mendoza turned up lookin' for the cattle.'

Ephraim was silent for a moment, then said in a low tone. 'There's somethin' funny goin' on around here, Lando. I've felt it for some time now. Those coyotes seem to know too much of our plans.'

Brad looked up sharply. 'You think there's somebody in the Flying Y crew passin' them information?'

'Could be. A cowpoke's pay ain't so big that he wouldn't trade information if the price was high enough.'

'If there is, then there's sure enough one way to find out,' replied the other musingly. 'All we got to do is spread around some false information. Whoever's behind all this wants to see

173

Callaghan broke, ain't much doubt about that. Most of the other ranchers have already been busted by these killers and they're bound to concentrate on him now. Far as I know, there's only Herb Thompson still workin' his place and they made a try for him night before last. I'll talk it over with Callaghan. This time, we might be ready for 'em in force and if we can catch 'em on the wrong foot we can smash 'em for good.'

Ephraim stepped back and surveyed his handiwork, nodding in satisfaction. 'Reckon that bandage ought to hold until it's healed.'

Brad got to his feet. As the little cowpuncher turned away, he said softly. 'I don't have to warn you to keep quiet about our conversation. I don't want anybody else to know of it except Callaghan.'

The other grinned. 'I know when to keep my mouth shut,' he said sombrely.

Brad waited for a moment, then moved over to Callaghan. The foreman was saying something in a low tone as he approached, then abruptly broke off and moved back towards the fire, picking up a couple of logs and tossing them on to the glowing embers, sending red sparks lifting high into the air.

'Feelin' any better, Brad?' inquired Callaghan concernedly.

'Sure.' Brad glanced round to make sure that none of the crew were in earshot, then said in a low tone: 'I'd like to put forward a plan to trap these rustlers, Jeb. I figure that if it works out, we might be able to stop 'em once and for all.'

'All right. Let's hear it.'

'The way I see it, there's somebody in the crew who's passin' word through to Forlan or Mendoza about the movement of your herd. They know just when and where to strike to achieve maximum surprise. If I'm right, then I suggest that you move the herd to some place well away from here, then put the word around where it is. You can bet your last dollar that those critters in

Mendaro will learn of it within twenty-four hours. Once we reckon they've had time to get the news, Flint and I will drive those steers back here, leavin' the rest of the boys holed up in the place where they're supposed to be. If you stick with the rest of the crew, you can keep an eye on 'em, make sure that nobody pulls out for any reason at all. I'll do the same with Flint. That way, nobody will know of the switch.'

'I find it hard to believe that there's a traitor in my crew.'

'It's somethin' you'll have to face up to sooner or later. Even on the pay you make, there's always somebody who aims to get more if he can. And Forlan will pay well if he's behind all this.'

'If one of my men is betrayin' me, I'll flay his hide off his back and then string up what's left of him.'

'We'll soon find out if you agree to do as I say. And not a word of this to any of the others.'

6

Betrayed!

Early the following morning, the herd moved out of the long lush valley and headed due north. Riding point, Brad swept his gaze over the men moving with the herd watching each one. So far, there had been no move by any of them to slip away from the camp, although all of them had been told that they were driving the cattle to a fresh spot where they would be out of reach of any rustlers, where it would be easier to defend them just in case Mendoza's men were more daring than they had figured and decided to push their luck to the limit.

As he rode, he felt the nagging sense of worry return. If he had been correct in his supposition, then someone would make a move very soon, would attempt to slip away without being seen and ride hell for leather to Mendaro. They followed a section of several miles where the grass had been dried out and withered by past droughts, where there was little, if any, water and the encroaching desert had begun to move in to reclaim the land which had been its own in past ages.

Not until they came near the river did the terrain change at all. Here, at times, the river overflowed its banks and regularly deposited a thick layer of silt which, beneath the grass, formed an extremely fertile soil where almost anything would flourish. Also, further to the north, there had once been a wide lake which had, some centuries before, dried out completely, leaving a huge, shallow depression, a vast saucer-shape in the ground.

It was here that they had decided to keep the herd until the time came to put the second part of his plan into operation. By late afternoon, with the pitiless sun still beating down over the wide prairie, the last of the strays had been rounded up and brought into the depression. The men made camp on the lee of the sloping bank between the herd and the river, settling down to their chores.

Around dark, Brad made his way up the slope towards one of the high ridges which overlooked the plain. The sun had already set and the last of the brilliant reds and oranges in the west was fading swiftly against the darkness of the onrushing night. Somewhere off in the distance, a coyote sent up an eerie wail, the sound running up and down a saw-edged scale, sending little shivers along his spine. It was strange, he reflected, how that lost, lonely sound always affected men in this way. Building himself a smoke, he pushed the cigarette between his lips, lit it and inhaled deeply.

A sudden movement at his back brought him whirling on his heel. Ephraim came up the slope. 'I thought you'd like to know that Winter's gone,' he said, wheezing a little with the exertion of the climb.

'You sure?' Brad snapped.

'Positive. Ain't no sign of him anywhere. I've checked with the rest of the boys. Nobody can recall seein' him durin' the afternoon. Last anyone saw him, he was ridin' point just before noon.'

'So.' Brad whistled softly. 'Looks as though we was right. Has the boss ridden in yet?'

'Should be here in an hour or so. He'll be bringin' in the rest of the men from the ranch.'

'Let me know when he comes. And not a word of this to anyone.'

The other rubbed the side of his nose with a horny finger. 'I'd have staked my life on Winter,' he said, puzzled. 'Hell! he's been with us for nearly five years now. One of the best wranglers and cowpokes in the business. I'd never have figured him to sell us out to Forlan.'

'Reckon you can never tell a skunk

from his colour,' Brad retorted. 'I'll circle around just in case somethin' happened to him. But it sure looks like he's our man.'

* * *

Cutting Big Jet out of the remuda, Brad climbed wearily into the saddle. It had been a long drive through the boiling heat of the day and the chances now were that there would be an equally long drive back. He did not doubt that Mendoza would soon know of the drive if he did not do so already. How long it would be before he acted was problematical. He might decide to strike that very night before they were ready for him, or he might even hold off for some days, making them sweat it out. But they could not afford to take any chances with the herd. It was imperative that they should drive it back to the line camp before morning. If they waited any longer, the risks were too great. Everything, he realized, depended on Mendoza staying true to form.

After circling the herd, he backtracked along the trail they had taken during the afternoon, eyes alert, searching for any sign of Winter. Inwardly, he was somewhat pleased at the way things had turned out. Yet he could not rid himself of the suspicion that all was not quite as it should be; that something was wrong. He rode steadily until he came to the river, moved along its bank in both directions, away from the place where they had forded it. Nowhere along the bank did he come across the trail left by a solitary rider. It certainly looked as though Winter had pulled out before they had hit the river. There was, of course, the possibility that he had ridden out with Callaghan to fetch the rest of the men from the ranch, but somehow he doubted it. Callaghan had said nothing of taking anyone with him.

Presently, he emerged on to a wide bench of rock, forced his way through a dense jungle of undergrowth which covered a long rise and found himself on the rimrock of a small basin. Before him, the ground sloped down steeply towards the shallow pool which gleamed faintly in the moonlight. On the far side, the ground lifted to an almost vertical wall of red sandstone, totally void of vegetation, ribbed and sparred by long ages of faulting and erosion. He let his gaze roam idly over the scene, then looked more intently. There were tracks in the soft earth around the rim of the pool and he leaned forward in the saddle, scanning them intently. They were recent; probably not more than a few hours old and they were the tracks of two horses.

The tracks led around the pool and, getting from the saddle, he found a half-smoked cigarette butt which had been ground into the dirt by a boot heel. Picking it out gently, he examined it in the flooding moonlight. There was no doubt about the brand. It came from north of the border, not the sort which he would have expected a Mexican to smoke.

Straightening up, he stared about him, brow knit in puzzlement. Had Winter come this way, he wondered. And if so, had he met someone here? During the drive, he had never thought to keep an eye on their back trail, knowing that in open country, none of the rustlers would dare approach close enough to give them any trouble. Evidently, he figured, they had been shadowed by at least two of Mendoza's men. It was the only plausible explanation.

Lifting his gaze, he saw something showing just above the ridge and thrust his way through the thorny undergrowth, clambering over rough-edged boulders, ignoring the raking of thorns against his flesh. Reaching the top, he raised his head slowly, an inch at a time. In the moonlight, the contours of the land grew out of the wide backdrop. There was a broken-down shack some thirty yards away, the roof sagging in on broken timbers, the door hanging open where the hinges had rusted away.

Easing the Colt from its holster, he padded forward, paused for a moment beside the door, then stepped inside swinging the Colt in a wide arc, his finger tight on the trigger, ready for trouble. Then he relaxed. The place was empty. The table was of rough deal, bare and covered by a thin layer of grey dust. The remains of a fire lay in the splintered hearth, but the ash was cold and clearly there had been no fire there for some time.

Stepping outside, he threw a quick glance towards the west, then glanced up at the moon, knew there would be no time to waste trying to follow that trail. Saddling up once more, he made his way back to the herd, found that Jeb Callaghan had arrived there half an hour earlier and was waiting impatiently for him.

'Where the hell have you been, Lando?' he asked harshly.

'Just out to see if I could find any sign of Winter.'

The other thinned down his lips across his teeth. 'You won't find any sign of that polecat,' he grated. 'He'll be in Mendaro now, spillin' all he knows to Mendoza.'

'Maybe. Are all of the others here?'

'Every last one o' them,' affirmed the rancher. 'I've given Flint his orders. He's to ride out with you and the herd. Better get 'em started. It's a long trail back to the line camp and I sure hope you know what you're doin'.'

Brad eyed the other closely. 'You're sure gettin' jitters all of a sudden,' he remarked.

'This is my herd that's at stake here. Wouldn't you get a mite uneasy in my place?'

'Maybe so.' Brad signalled to Flint and the foreman stepped up into the saddle, checking the Winchester before thrusting it into the scabbard.

Slowly, the herd began to move under their prompting. The great beasts were still weary, stubborn, raising their voices to the starlit heavens in protest at a night drive. Fortunately, Flint was an experienced hand at this game and once the leaders had been eased out of the milling mass, they made good headway, reaching the river and splashing across it.

Swinging around the rear of the drag, Brad scanned the horizon continually, watching for any sign of trouble. They had deliberately chosen a circuitous trail back to the camp so as to reduce the risk of bumping into the outlaws. He and his mount were both tired after the long day and he allowed Big Jet to pick its own pace, riding some quarter of a mile from the slow-moving cattle.

Flint was on the far side of the herd, equally watchful, urging the steers along, evidently anxious to be off the range and back at camp. The moon came up and a brisk wind whipped over the range; a chilling, biting wind. Out of the edge of his vision, Brad saw several stragglers behind the main bunch and wheeled his mount sharply. He had almost reached them when Big Jet shied suddenly, skidded to an abrupt halt, almost unseating his rider.

Clinging tightly to the reins, Brad muttered a sharp oath, then cast about him for some indication of the cause of his mount's fright. At first, he could see nothing, figured it might have been a rattler which had slithered back among the rocks. Then, shifting his gaze slightly, he made out the patch of darker shadow some five yards away, among a cluster of rocks. He dismounted quickly, ran forward. The body was wedged tightly between two of the boulders which studded the ground and it was not an easy job to move it. Pulling the corpse loose, he stretched it out on the rough ground, turning the dead man over. A faint gust of surprise crossed his features as he stared down into the upturned face. It was Winter!

A brief examination told him that the other had been shot in the back from fairly close range. Both of his guns still reposed in their holsters and evidently the other had been taken completely by surprise, without a chance to defend himself. Slowly, he straightened up, a sharp sense of apprehension assailing him as the full implications of his discovery came to him.

It was not difficult to see that the other had been dead for some little time and equally obvious was the fact that he could not have been the crew member they had suspected of betraying them to the rustlers. Yet why should anyone want to kill Winter? Unless it was to throw them off the scent, to make them believe that he was the traitor among the Flying Y crew. Back in the saddle, he rode round the running herd until he came up with Flint.

'We've got to get this herd bottled up — and quick!' he called, raising his voice to make himself heard above the thunder of the cattle.

'Somethin' wrong?'

'Plenty. I found Winter. He's back

189

there with a slug between his shoulders. Must've been shot some hours ago.'

'Hell. Then that means — '

'It means we've been outsmarted. Mendoza knows of our plans all right, only the way I see it, he knows everythin'.'

The foreman did not need any further explanation of the seriousness of the situation. Kicking spurs into his horse's flanks, he urged the animal towards the rear of the herd, whipping his Colt from its holster, firing it into the air. Brad swung quickly around towards the far side of the running steers, cutting across their path, bent low in the saddle, ignoring the flashing horns which passed within inches of him. Several times, he was almost run down in the mad rush of muscle and sinew as the herd began to run. Their wariness forgotten in the din of gunfire that bellowed in their ears, they surged forward in a vast, shadowed wave across the plains, following the natural leaders as the two men fought to turn them in the direction of the camp.

* * *

The floorboards of the hut creaked dismally as Brad paced towards the narrow window. Their luck had held so far and the herd was now in the lee of the low ridge which bordered the small camp. How long it would continue to be on their side, he did not know. Men who spend their lives in an atmosphere of danger and peril develop a sixth sense, an instinct, which warns them of oncoming danger before it comes and Brad had that feeling now.

There was a movement outside and Flint came in, closing the door behind him, trailing the Winchester in his right hand. He set the weapon down on the table.

'No sign of any trouble as yet,' he grunted. 'One good thing, those steers are so bone weary after all that drivin', they won't be easily spooked.'

Brad shrugged his shoulders. 'If Mendoza knows that there are only the two of us here and the rest of the crew are fifteen miles away, he won't let that little detail bother him. He only has to finish us off and he can afford to take his time.' Idly, he wondered just who the traitor might be. Whoever it was, he had played a smart game from start to finish. The fact that he had succeeded in killing Winter without being noticed, testified to that. Almost certainly, the killer had been someone that Winter knew and trusted, otherwise he would have at least made an attempt to defend himself.

'If I could just get my hands on the critter who killed Winter and landed us in this trouble, I'd — '

'Save your recriminations for later,' Brad advised. 'If we're to stay alive, we'd better have some plan ready for when they do attack us.'

'You seem damn sure they'll come soon.'

'I reckon you can bet on that. Now, you know this country better than I do. Which way are they likely to come?'

The foreman rubbed his stubbled

chin. 'They'll ride out from town, that much is for sure. That means they'll have to cross the boundary fence to the east unless they make a detour around towards the south, and that ain't likely. It would take 'em miles out of their way.'

'And there's only the one gate in that direction,' mused Brad thoughtfully. 'And I can't see 'em breakin' through that wire. Too much trouble for men like that, particularly if they know they won't face much opposition.'

Flint frowned and wiped the palms of his hands on his pants. 'So they'll cut in through the twin buttes yonder.'

Brad nodded. 'There maybe another way, but that seems the most obvious.' He moved towards the door. 'You got any dynamite here?'

'Dynamite? Used to be some when Callaghan was blasting a channel from the river a couple of years back. Ain't seen it for a while, though. If there's any still around it'll be in the shed yonder.'

'See if you can lay your hands on it. There might be just a chance that we can even the odds a little.'

The other was gone for the best part of ten minutes. When he returned, there was a wooden box in his arms. He set it down carefully on the table, well away from the solitary lamp. Inserting the blade of his knife beneath the lid, Brad prised it off. There were ten or a dozen yellow sticks of explosive at the bottom. He lifted them out carefully, laid them side by side on the table.

'This should be enough to cause some trouble to those killers.'

'Mendoza will be after the whole herd this time,' observed the other. 'You might stop a few of 'em, but there ain't sufficient explosive there to do much damage.'

Brad grinned tightly. 'Reckon that all depends on where this dynamite is placed. Come with me and keep me covered in case they show up before we're ready.'

★   ★   ★

The moon vanished behind a thick
layer of cloud and Brad was forced to
work in almost total darkness. Beneath
his fingers, the hard rock gradually
splintered into sharp-edged shards as
he hammered away at it with the small
pick. He worked as quickly as he dared,
knowing that time was now precious.
The night was wearing on and unless
he was mistaken, those killers from
Mendaro would show up at any time.
He was standing on a narrow ledge
some forty feet above the floor of the
valley where it ran between the two
sky-rearing buttes; a ledge barely more
than three feet in width, giving him
scarcely any room at all in which to
work. Somewhere below him, at the
mouth of the canyon, he knew Flint was
watching the open plain to the east,
alert for the first sign of movement
from that direction.

Slowly, the hole widened and deep-
ened under his insistent hammering.

His arms and shoulders were aching intolerably with the strain and sweat ran down his forehead into his eyes, half-blinding him although now, with the moonlight gone, it made very little difference. He was forced to work more by feel than sight.

When he judged that it was some eighteen inches in depth, he paused, wiped the sweat from his face with the back of his sleeve, then bent his legs slowly, clinging like a limpet to the sheer rock face. This was going to be the tricky, dangerous bit. The dynamite was old and had a greasy feel which meant that it was far more sensitive than normal. One wrong move and he could blow himself to kingdom come. Steadying himself, he reached for the remaining sticks, placed them carefully in the hole he had hewn out of the rock, packing them as tightly together as he dared. Now there was only the long length of fuse to put in place and everything would be ready.

He had already burned a short

length, knew how long it would take for the forty-five foot length to burn through. Gently, he inserted the detonator into the last stick of explosive, looped a length of fuse around an outjutting piece of rock, securely in place, then he let the rest of the fuse drop into the valley.

Clambering down into the canyon, he laid the fuse out, ready to be lit, then joined Flint. The other was seated on an outcrop of rock, his Winchester between his knees.

'No sign of 'em yet,' he said tersely. 'Could be you were wrong about Winter's killin'.'

'I wouldn't bet on it.'

There was little to see over in the east; still less to hear. The two men waited, feeling the faint prickling of danger, straining their ears. Then, softly, far off, there came the sound they had been waiting for, the faint drumming of hoofbeats, and to senses trained in such intangibles, the noise was readily apparent even though the riders must have been the best part of five miles away. Brad froze with his back to the cliff, breath held in check, touching the foreman's arm. But the other had already picked out the sound, gave a quick nod and shifted his position.

'You sure you know what you're doin' with that dynamite?' he asked gruffly.

'I'd better be.' Brad eased himself upright, began moving back between the towering walls of sandstone. Everything now depended upon those men following the trail between the buttes. If they didn't; then all of his preparations would have been in vain.

Judging by the sounds, there were plenty of men in the oncoming party. The newcomers were swinging steadily in their direction, riding boldly and making little effort to conceal their approach, utterly confident in their superior numbers. He smiled grimly to himself in the darkness.

Crouching down beside the spot

where the thin thread of fuse ran up the sheer face of the butte, he motioned Flint to take up his position among the rocks well out of danger. He estimated that the men were now less than a mile away, still holding to their steady pace. The trouble now was that in the darkness, the sense of hearing could prove deceptive. He held motionless, the matches in his hand, barely breathing. The moon was moving now in its long glide across the heavens. Soon it would be near the zenith, throwing its light directly down into the canyon, lighting up all of the dark shadows.

Slowly, the seconds ticked by and now the drumming of hoofs on the hard ground was clearly audible. A few moments later, he was able to pick out the riders in the moonlight, waited tensely for a further fifteen seconds, then struck the match and applied the flame to the end of the fuse, shielding it with his cupped hands. The trail of powder caught, sputtered, then began to burn with only the faint wisp of smoke to indicate that it was still alight.

He paused for only a moment, then ran back among the rocks. Out of the corner of his eye, he caught a glimpse of the foreman crouched in a notch in the rocks, his face a pale blur in the moonlight. Then there was no time to notice anything else. Flinging himself forward, he pulled himself under cover at the end of the canyon, whipping the Colt from its holster.

The dark mass of the riders swept forward towards the far end of the canyon. Briefly, Brad wondered whether Mendoza himself was leading them. Clenching his teeth until the muscles of his jaw ached with the strain, he stared off into the darkness. The first bunch of men had already entered the canyon, were threading their way forward. Very soon now, they would be in line with that slowly-burning length of fuse.

Had the fuse continued to burn? If so, how close was that tiny red spark to the tightly-packed explosive? The first five men passed the spot, the rest moving up close behind. He felt the sweat break out anew on his forehead; trickling down into his eyes. If they all managed to get past, everything would be lost. He moved forward a little, bringing up the Colt. Maybe there was just one chance to halt them long enough.

His finger tightened on the trigger as he laid the sights on the leading rider. Then, before he could exert the final ounce of pressure, all hell erupted. The vivid red flash of the explosion was followed by the titanic wave of concussion, succeeded in turn by the cavernous rumble of hundreds of tons of solid rock on the move.

The entire side of the butte came away, surging outward under the force of the explosion. Brad had a confused glimpse of great boulders, torn loose from the canyon wall, plunging down towards the tightly packed riders directly in the path of the avalanche.

The shrill screams of the doomed men were lost in the thunder of the rockfall as the slowly atrophying echoes of the detonation died away into the distance.

Most of the men in the centre of the column were blotted out in that moment of red-edged fury. Half a dozen or so at the head of the mass had managed to spur their mounts forward in time to escape being crushed and it was possible that some of the stragglers had fared likewise. But undoubtedly the main group of men had been killed outright, for surely no man could have survived that terrible blast and rockfall.

In the darkness and confusion, the leading riders urged their mounts along the narrow trail, anxious to be free of the canyon, not knowing whether a second charge might have been laid, ready to detonate within minutes.

Brad allowed them to come on, then deliberately stood up, exposing himself, the Colt in the fist belching smoke and flame. He saw two of the men go down, spinning from the saddle as the lead took them full in the chest. The others bent low in the saddle to present more difficult targets, realizing now the full extent of the trap into which they had unwittingly ridden. On the far side of the opening, Flint poured a steady stream of well aimed rifle fire into them. A third man suddenly released his hold on the reins, tumbled sideways, his boot caught in the stirrup, head and shoulders trailing over the uneven ground as his mount raced on.

Brad threw a swift glance along the canyon. The fall had almost completely blocked it some five hundred yards away and it would take time for survivors on the far side to work their way around. It was time to move and head back for the camp where he and Flint had agreed to make a stand.

The men still in the saddle were wheeling their mounts desperately, circling back as they fought to bring the panicky animals under control. Running doubled up, he headed for the huts. Stilettos of red flame lanced out of the darkness and he heard the pecking of slugs among the rocks around his feet as he raced forward. They had cut down the opposition, but the battle was not yet won. He reckoned that there were probably fifteen or so of the enemy still alive and it was only a matter of time before they collected themselves and recovered from their surprise.

Reaching the door of the nearest adobe hut, he flung himself inside. Less than ten seconds later, Flint followed him across the threshold, throwing himself to one side of the door as Brad slammed it shut and thrust the bar into place. Breathing heavily, he moved to the window and peered out into the moonlight.

'Hell! But that sure finished most of 'em,' grunted the foreman. 'That was somethin' they never expected.'

'There are still enough of 'em left in the saddle to make a fight of it if they've a mind to,' Brad reminded him grimly.

'Could be that if we can hold out

until dawn, there might be a chance of Callaghan and the rest of the boys showin' up. When they ain't attacked, they might figure on it bein' a double-cross and head this way.'

'It's a possibility, but not one on which I'd like to stake my life.'

The other thrust fresh shells into the repeater, checked the mechanism, then laid the rifle near the window and went over to the rack on the wall, bringing a second Winchester and a box of shells which he laid on the ground beside him. 'At least we can cover the herd from here,' he remarked. 'They won't find it easy to sneak past us and spook them steers. 'Specially now that they're so goddamn tired after the two drives.'

Brad lifted a hand, pointed. 'There are the rest of 'em.'

In the moonlight, they made out the straggling band of riders who came into view around the corner of the buttes. The three men who had earlier ridden out of the canyon, rode up to meet the main band and for a while the rustlers stood off in the distance, making no move, evidently debating their next course of action.

'You reckon they're figurin' on rushin' us?' muttered Flint.

'Seems more'n likely. How else would you figure a bunch like that to react now that we've killed half of 'em?'

Flint nodded, but said nothing more, settling himself more comfortably behind the window, the Winchester cradled in his hands. The moon went in behind a trailing bank of cloud and in the same instant, as if they had been waiting for that moment, the bunch of riders spurred their mounts in the direction of the camp, firing as they came on. Brad picked out the leaden thud of bullets against the thick adobe walls, sent up a silent prayer for their thickness, then smashed out the glass in front of him, thrusting the barrel of the Colt through the splintered opening and began shooting, switching targets as soon as he saw a man fall from the saddle.

Pandemonium reigned for long minutes. As they neared the hut, the riders fanned out, pumping slugs in from all angles, hoping that the weight of their fire, if not its accuracy, would enable some of the bullets to find their mark. Flint triggered off shot after shot in rapid succession, the hammer blows sounding like a trip hammer in the confined space until Brad's ears throbbed with the racket.

There was something fanatical in the way the riders came on, apparently ignoring the hail of lead which tore into their ranks. Then Brad saw the reason. Behind the foremost wave of riders, came two others, bearing lighted torches in their hands. He threw a swift glance about the room. There was no danger at all of the thick adobe walls catching fire. But the flat roof was a totally different matter, being constructed of dry timber.

'Get those men with the torches,' he yelled harshly.

Flint had already seen the danger.

Cursing volubly under his breath, he raised the rifle, sent a shot towards the racing men, flinching a little as a keyholing bullet whined through the window and smashed into the wall at their backs. His shot missed and as Brad let the hammer of the Colt go beneath his thumb, he heard the dull click as it fell on an empty chamber.

The main weight of gunfire had now shifted towards the sides of the hut where it struck ineffectually against the thick walls. Crouching down, he plucked fresh cartridges from the loops in his belt, thrust them into the gun with stiff fingers. Flint was ramming shells into the breech of the Winchester at the same time, occasionally lifting his head to peer out at the oncoming riders.

Spinning the chambers of the Colt, Brad pushed himself up on to his knees, aimed swiftly, sighting the nearer gunman. He loosed off a trio of shots, the echoes blurring into a single roll of sound. The man arched abruptly in the saddle, swung up his arm in a spasmodic jerk of shoulder muscles and with his last ounce of strength in his body, threw the torch towards the shack. It fell short into the yard, spluttering, sending a shower of red sparks skittering across the ground as the breeze caught them.

Twisting, he fired at the second half-breed. The other was now less than twenty yards away, standing straight in the saddle, his legs braced in the stirrups. Brad's first, hurried, shot missed completely as the other jerked his mount around with his free hand. At the same time, the blazing pine torch arced through the air above the line of Brad's vision. Kicking heels into his horse's flanks, the other urged his mount away. The darkness was spattered by winking flashes of red and he could see that the rest of the bunch had sneaked in close.

Pressing himself tightly against the wall, Brad fired at running shadows that passed across his vision, blurred shapes in the tantalising moonlight. A man screamed in mortal agony, dropped his gun and buckled at the knees, clutching at his chest as he went down. Flint emptied his rifle, dropped back on to his haunches to reload, then suddenly lifted his head, staring up at the ceiling. Thin wisps of smoke were eddying into the room and the smell of burning assailed their nostrils.

'Hellfire! That torch must've landed on the roof.'

The roof was beginning to burn as the flames bit into the dry wood. Brad thinned his lips. This was something he hadn't bargained for. If that fire succeeded in gaining a firm hold the entire roof would come in and they faced the choice of being roasted alive or running out into the massed fire of the outlaws. It was one hell of a decision to have to make.

He drew himself up a little as a harsh voice from outside, yelled: 'Better come on out, *amigos*. Very soon you burn.'

Brad could feel the heat of the flames

on the back of his neck. The smoke was getting thicker now, rolling down from the blazing timbers overhead. He took a deep breath, tightened his lips grimly. There was a wide patch of fire in the far corner of the room where part of the roof was hanging from the supports.

'Is there any back way out of here?' he asked tightly.

Flint shook his head. 'Wouldn't make any difference if there was. They'll have men all around the place by now. We'll be sittin' ducks the minute we try to make a run for it.'

'You got any further ideas?'

Outside, the rustlers evidently figured that the call for them to surrender had fallen on deaf ears, for a sudden tornado of gunfire broke out. One of the windows crashed into the room, showering Brad with shards of glass. Brushing it off his jacket, he squirmed across the floor, keeping his head well down as bullets sang through the air above him. Freezing just beneath the window, he remained motionless while the storm of lead crashed into the room, then risked a quick glance into the darkness. He could just make out the place where the main force were concentrated. Most of them had dismounted now, were crouched down, ready for them to make their break.

The smoke was thicker now, billowing out through the shattered windows, filling the room to the point where every breath was an agonizing torture. Brad's head felt oddly light and there was a pounding in his temples at the back of his eyes.

Grabbing the foreman by the arm, he said harshly: 'There's just one chance, Flint. That smoke is drifting across towards the store yonder. If we can get through the door and into it, we might stand a chance.'

'That ain't no chance at all,' rasped the other.

'It's the only one we've got. Take it or leave it.' Brad moved to the door, lifted down the wooden bar. Checking that every chamber in the Colt was filled, he signalled to the foreman. Reluctantly, the other got to his feet and joined him. Fighting for breath, Brad waited while the firing outside died down, then heaved the door open with all of his strength, at the same time thrusting himself forward over the rock-strewn ground, body bent double. The smoke swirled all about him. Once he stumbled, almost fell headlong as his feet slipped from under him.

A sudden yell went up. They had been seen. Almost as if it had been a signal, the gunfire broke out again and he dimly made out the thunder of hoofs as some men spurred their mounts towards them. All at once, the comparative safety of the store seemed a long way off. Worse still, the smoke petered out some thirty yards or so from the other building. A chill went through him as he realized that they had committed themselves to an act which was little short of sheer suicide. But there was nothing for it now but to go on. There could be no turning back.

At the very edge of his vision, he glimpsed three riders bearing down on him. Muzzle flashes blossomed blue-crimson in the moonlit dimness. The vicious hum of lead close to his head spurred him on to still greater efforts. He was less than ten yards from the store when he heard Flint cry out behind him. Checking his stride, he glanced back. The foreman had been hit in the leg, had gone down in a sprawling heap. Jerking up his Colt, he fired swiftly at the riders, now so close that he could make out their leering faces beneath the wide-brimmed hats. Two men were pitched from their saddles before they realized their danger. The third came on, grinning viciously. A bullet plucked at Brad's sleeve; a second punched a hole in his hat brim, almost tearing it from his head. Then the Colt in Brad's hand spoke for a third time.

A dark hole, like a shadow, appeared between the rustler's eyes. The impact snapped him upright in the saddle, legs straight in the stirrups. The horse reared sharply, throwing the rider off. The man was dead before his body hit the dirt.

Brad did not wait to see whether there were any other men advancing on him. Bending, he hauled Flint across his shoulders, staggering the rest of the way into the store, where he lowered the foreman on to the straw-covered floor, running back to the door and going down on one knee, thrusting shells into the Colt.

Flint came crawling across, dragging his injured leg. As Brad looked round at him, he grunted through clenched teeth: 'Hell! I can still fire this rifle at them critters out yonder. How far d'you reckon you'll get on your own?'

Brad grinned back at the other. At least the man had guts. He turned his attention back to the rustlers. At that very moment, the blazing roof of the adobe hut fell in with a cavernous roar, lighting up the scene, picking out the small group of running figures. The rustlers, disgruntled and enraged at their failure to finish the two men, were now taking no chances. There were probably ten of them still on their feet and they were swinging around in an attempt to attack from three sides. With Flint lying on his belly beside him, Brad commenced firing into the advancing men.

7

Hot Triggers

A sudden roar of deafening gunfire broke from the approaching gunmen. Bullets ploughed through the wooden walls of the store. Brad winced as a splinter sliced through the cloth of his jacket, drawing blood from his shoulder. Flint's rifle flamed in two lightning shots that were blended into one. A man screamed and toppled sideways, swayed drunkenly for a moment, then went down. Two more jerked, threw up their arms and fell back into the dust. Then the remaining men were running back for cover.

'Hold your fire,' Brad yelled, as Flint raised the Winchester again. 'They'll be bankin' on us usin' up all our ammunition. Then they can come in and take us without any trouble.'

217

Silence fell over the camp. In the moonlight, it was just possible to make out the shapes of the men in the distance. Evidently they were quite prepared to wait things out; almost as though they knew that there was no hope for the two men trapped in the store.

'Looks like we just jumped clear out of the fryin' pan and into the proverbial fire,' Flint muttered. He shifted his position a little, grimacing as pain jarred through his injured leg.

'They ain't got so many men left that they can afford to take foolish chances,' Brad remarked. 'Looks like they're goin' to have a little conference to decide which way they'll finish us.' He motioned with the barrel of the Colt to where the rustlers were clustered in a small group, heads down, out of range of his own gun, although whether or not the Winchester might just reach them, and whether it might then be possible to get in a killing shot at that distance, he did not know.

Then he spotted something else which brought a stirring of hope to him. Swiftly, he leaned over, took the Winchester from Flint's startled grasp.

'Over there,' he said shortly. 'About ten yards from those men. Unless I'm mistaken, that's the box you took that dynamite from, ain't it?'

The foreman squinted into the moonlight, then sucked in a sharp intake of air. 'By Hades, you're right. You figure you can hit it from here?'

'With a bit of luck, it's possible. Though whether a bullet will set it off, I wouldn't like to say.' Stretching himself full length on the straw, he sighted along the barrel, found the squat shape of the wooden box in the sights, waited for a moment, then squeezed the trigger, working the mechanism swiftly as he pumped two more shots into the small target.

The rustlers were on the point of rising to their feet and moving forward when the night was abruptly shattered by the detonating blast of the explosive.

Tricky stuff at the best of times, in its present unstable condition, the impact of a well-placed bullet, hammering into it at high velocity, had been sufficient to detonate it. Brad had a confused impression of men being hurled sideways like rag dolls, tossed into the air as if seized by invisible hands.

Ears throbbing from the concussive detonation wave, Brad saw a handful of survivors racing back for their mounts. The rest were mere humps of dark shadow, unmoving on the ground. Getting to his feet, he sent a couple of ineffectual shots after the fleeing riders, then went back to Flint. The foreman had pushed himself up into a sitting position, was trying to staunch the flow of blood from the deep wound in his leg.

'Better lie still while I put a tourniquet on that.' Twisting his kerchief, he tied it around the other's leg above the wound. Gradually, the bleeding lessened.

'Any sign of the rest of them

coyotes?' grunted Flint thickly.

'After what just happened, I doubt if they'll stop runnin' until they're back in Mendaro or across the Mexican border.'

'I sure hope you're right.' Flint got to his feet with the other helping him.

★　★　★

The rest of the Flying Y came into the camp early the following morning. Surveying the scene of carnage, Callaghan said thinly. 'I'd sure like to know just how they managed to find out what we'd planned. To my way of thinking it had to be Winter.'

Brad drew deeply on his cigarette, let the smoke trickle out in little pinches through his nostrils before answering. 'It wasn't Winter who betrayed our plan. He's dead. Somebody met up with him durin' the drive yesterday, lured him off the trail and then put a slug into his back.'

The rancher's wintry features held no

humour. 'You sure of that, Brad?'

'I found him yesterday. He'd been dead for some hours.'

'So we're back where we started. It could be anyone.'

'I don't see it that way.'

Jeb Callaghan's lips thinned. 'Indeed! What makes you say that?'

'Because as far as we know, everybody else in the crew has been accounted for now that we've eliminated Winter.'

'Go on.'

'So they must've found out some other way. Maybe had men trailin' us every minute, reportin' back on our movements.'

'At least the herd's safe.' Callaghan turned to survey the cattle, now grazing peacefully in the long valley. Then he switched his gaze to the bodies scattered around the buildings. 'As for these critters, I'll detail some men to bury 'em.'

'If you've got nothin' else in mind for me at present, I think I'll scout around, just in case those outlaws left someone behind to keep an eye on the place.'

'You sure you feel up to it?' queried the other. 'You can't have had more'n a few hours' sleep in three days.'

'I'll make out,' Brad said. Nodding to the rest of the men, he went over to Big Jet, tightened the cinch under the stallion's belly, then swung up into leather.

The sun was just lifting clear of the horizon as he circled the line camp before heading south. After what had happened during the night, he doubted if any of the Mexicans would be hanging around the place, but it would be unwise to take any chances. Whoever was at the back of the attempt to grab off all this land for himself would not let the loss of those men stop him for long.

He rode for a couple of hours, cutting over to the boundary fence, passing through it into the more inhospitable country that lay beyond. Before him lay the desert, stretching clear to the Mexican border. In the harsh sun glare it looked grim and forbidding.

As he rode, he digested all that had occurred over the past few days, trying to make some sense out of it, to see the underlying threat of circumstance which must surely be there. But the more he puzzled over it, the more chaotic everything seemed to be, with no connecting links between events. He was beginning to understand, for the first time, the bitter feuds that existed along this gun-torn frontier country.

When high noon came, with the Texas sun burning down upon him with a tangible pressure that ate deep into his bones, he found himself a small camp site where a narrow, sluggish stream meandered between alkali dunes. The water held an acrid taste, but it slaked his thirst and he allowed Big Jet to drink his fill as he huddled himself into the shade of a stunted stand of brush and built himself a smoke, his hat brim tilted forward over his eyes. Sweat stained his shirt, chafing his flesh with every movement he made.

Finishing the cigarette, he settled his shoulders back against the upthrusting column of sandstone that poked itself like some decayed tooth from the desert, closed his eyes and surrendered himself to the utter weariness in his body. He had long since trained himself to sleep for a few hours during the daytime, having grown accustomed to the curious inversion of light and dark.

When he woke, the sun was dipping swiftly towards the reddening western horizon and the long blue shadows lay over the land. As yet, there was no let-up in the blistering heat-head and he lay motionless for several minutes, listening to the crackle of the wind in the dry, skeletal branches of the mesquite. A few yards away, Big Jet lifted his head abruptly, scenting the wind, began pawing nervously at the ground. Weariness gave way to an alert caution. The stallion would scent trouble much earlier than he could and he had learned from past experience never to disregard signs such as this. Carefully, he came to his knees, loosing the Colt in its holster, straining his ears to pick out any sound which might have startled his mount.

Dusk was in the air; on the lower reaches, the night was already pushing away the last vestiges of day with a clustering of shadow. As he moved, the breeze brought to him the stealthy scrape of a boot against rock. Swinging sharply, his right hand dropped towards the butt of the Colt. Then he froze as shock coursed through him. The muzzle of a rifle was levelled on him from a few feet away. Behind the gun, his face leering evilly at him, stood Crawley.

Brad's earlier feeling — that Crawley was as cold a killer as any of Mendoza's men — appeared fully justified now. Even as he stared up at the other, more men appeared from among the rocks.

'Go ahead if you want to make a try

for your gun, Lando,' invited Crawley, his voice dry. 'Make your play.'

Brad shook his head, forced evenness into his tone. 'I'm not that big a fool.'

The gunhawk grinned, a mere thinning of his lips. 'I've been wonderin' just what sort of man you really are.'

'You'll find that out someday.'

'That don't seem likely. You put your spoke into things that don't concern you once too often. You won't get another chance, I can promise you that. Now get on your feet.'

Brad did not argue the point. To disobey with Crawley would simply hasten the other's pull on the trigger and he knew that a man such as this would kill without any compunction at all.

'Unbuckle your gunbelt and let it fall. Slowly. The first move you make that I don't like will be your last. Believe me, if it was up to me I'd kill you here and now.'

Brad did as he was told, kept his gaze

fixed on the other's face as one of the half-breeds stepped forward and picked up the gunbelt, slinging it over his shoulder. Brad let his breath go in a faint exhalation. Now that he knew that he was not to be killed at that very moment, he could afford to think and plan ahead, to wait for an opportunity to make a move as soon as the chance presented itself.

★   ★   ★

The trail they followed took them high into the scrubland which ran along the wide bench of ground fronting the hills. Sitting tautly upright in the saddle, his hands tied behind his back, Brad fought to maintain his balance as his captors forced the pace, eager to reach their destination. Whether they figured that some of the Flying Y might be roaming around, Brad was not sure. In spite of the rough jolting his body received, he managed to keep a tight look out on his surroundings, watching for landmarks which might head him back to wherever they were headed if he ever did get the chance to escape from these men.

At the moment, his future did not look too bright, but he had been in tight spots before and always clung to the adage that there was always a chance so long as he remained alive. The moon lay hidden behind a bank of thick cloud, but much of the sky remained clear and he was able to follow their general direction by the stars.

He reckoned it was a little after nightfall when the man in the lead reined up his mount and they came to a halt a quarter of a mile from a narrow V-shaped pass which slashed a deep cut through the high wall of rock. Crawley rode up alongside.

'Get down, Lando,' he ordered brusquely. 'We go the rest of the way on foot. One of the men will take your horse.'

Narrow-eyed and alert, he looked about him. The men were drawn up in a loose line. Not a chance of getting away without collecting a bullet for his pains. Shrugging resignedly, he slipped one leg over the saddle and dropped loosely to the ground, staggering a little off balance. One of the men said something harshly in Spanish and the others laughed raucously.

Their route lay up the steep hillside, along a track which was scarcely visible in the clinging darkness. Judging from the way they moved, he guessed that these men had travelled this way many times, knew every obstacle in the path. Feet slipping on the treacherous ground, he struggled forward, skirting the boulders which thrust themselves up in front of him without warning. Reaching the pass, they moved over a ragged-edged crest, then down the far side, going deeper into the hills. A few moments later, the moon sailed clear of the intruding cloud and he was able to see more clearly.

A faint glow came from somewhere directly ahead, but for a long moment he was unable to pinpoint its source.

Then, as they rounded a bend in the trail, he made out the mouth of a cave in the solid rock, saw that the light came from a fire which had been built just inside. In the flickering glow, the silhouettes of several men danced over the rough rock wall and there was a bunch of horses tethered to stakes almost out of sight on the far side of the cave.

So this was their hide-out. Now that they had brought him this far, he felt certain they could not afford to let him escape. A man moved out into the open as they approached.

'That you, Crawley?'

Brad recognised Sheriff Kerdy's voice, felt a tiny shock of surprise pass through him even though he had long since known that the lawman was working with these men.

'Of course it is — who the hell did you expect?' grated the other.

'Sorry. Didn't mean to — ' The other stepped on one side as Crawley thrust him out of the way.

'Trouble with you is, you never seem to do anythin' but look after your own miserable hide. If you'd only carried out your orders like you was told, this hombre would've been swingin' from a rope now and all of this trouble could have been averted. As it is, we've lost a heap of good men because of him.'

'Now see here, Crawley,' blustered Kerdy, his face flushing in the firelight. 'You got no call for remarks like that. I don't take my orders from you.'

'You do exactly as I say if you know what's good for you, Kerdy. I figure you've rested that carcass of yours long enough. Get up there into the rocks and relieve Jed.'

Kerdy stared at the gunman with narrowed eyes for a long moment, then turned savagely on his heel and made his way through the rocks. Crawley waited until the diminishing echo of the other's footsteps had died away into silence, then prodded Brad in the small of the back with his gun barrel, thrusting him inside the cave.

A savage kick in the ribs sent him sprawling on his face in the far corner of the cave. He felt rough rock tear at his cheek as he fell, felt the stab of pain roar through his skull. Then he rolled over and came up against the rock wall, breathing heavily as he waited for the agony to subside a little. Taking no further notice of him, Crawley went over to the fire and seated himself with the rest of the men, his back to Brad.

Sucking air down into his aching lungs, Brad thrust his legs out straight in front of him and turned his head slowly to survey his situation. There were six men seated around the fire and another couple near the wide entrance. How many were on guard outside he did not know. Possibly there were fifteen, maybe as many as twenty, men here he decided. Against the far wall, on the opposite side of the fire, several rifles were propped against the rock and several saddles had been thrown down in a heap close by. A couple of coffee pots stood on top of a smoke-blackened slab of stone and the sight of them made him realise just how thirsty he was.

Straightening up, he shouted. 'You got any coffee to spare, Crawley? Or are you waitin' for me to die of thirst?'

Without turning, Crawley eased himself to his feet, went over to the rock, picked up one of the coffee pots and came towards him.

'You want some coffee, Lando,' he snarled viciously. 'All right then, you can have some.'

He held the pot out in an outstretched hand. The wolfish grin stayed on his features as if it had been painted there. Even though Brad guessed the other's intention, there was nothing he could do about it. Tilting the pot, the other deliberately poured the hot liquid over his upturned face. Fortunately, it had been standing for some time, otherwise he would have been scalded. As it was, the coffee was hot enough to burn his flesh and with a gasp of pain, he twisted his head away, his ears filled with the harsh laughter of the rest of the men at the fire.

Brad glared up at the sneering face of the killer, shook his head to clear it. 'I'll remember that, Crawley,' he muttered thinly.

'You'll be clear into hell before you can do anythin' about it,' retorted the other, moving back to the fire.

Brad hauled himself up against the rock, tested the bonds which bound his wrists. The tough rope did not yield an inch and the man who had tied the knots had made a good job of it. The only thing to do now was to settle back and await events, not to waste his strength in a futile effort to free himself.

Several of the men around the fire had brought out whisky bottles, were passing them around, getting steadily drunker as the night passed. Easing his shoulders against the wall of the cave, Brad watched them closely from half-closed eyes, seeming to be asleep. His arms were becoming cramped and he shifted around slightly, sucked in a quick breath as a razor-sharp edge of rock dug deeply into the small of his back. Sitting up, moving as slowly and quietly as possible, he felt along it with his fingers. It was only a small protuberance, jutting out from the wall less than an inch. But it was enough for his purpose. Still keeping his eyes on the gunhawks around the fire, he began sawing away at it with his bonds, gritting his teeth as the sharp rock bit into his wrists. At the end of an hour, he had the satisfaction of finding the rawhide giving just a little.

By now, most of the men were stretched out on the floor of the cave much the worse for drink, snoring vigorously. Working steadily at the bonds, and pausing at intervals, feeling the blood running down his hands, he finally succeeded in breaking them. Outside, he noticed the first faint greyness of the dawn and knew that he would soon have to make his move if he was to have any chance at all. His gunbelt lay on the ground within easy reach of Crawley's hand, the Colt still reposing in the holster. Gently, he flexed his fingers and shoulders, bringing some of the feeling back into his muscles.

Once he got his hands on the gun, he might have a chance of getting out of the cave. But there were still those guards up in the rocks somewhere. Slowly, moving his limbs an inch at a time, he rose to his feet, ignoring the pain which darted through him. Wiping his hands on his pants, he edged forward, treading warily. One of the men rolled over on to his side, muttered something under his breath and he stiffened mechanically, tensed abruptly, then moved on again as the other drifted back to sleep.

Reaching down, scarcely breathing, he caught hold of the gunbelt, heard it scrape slightly on the rock. Swiftly now, he slung it around his middle, fastened the buckle, then eased the Colt from leather, checking the chambers. Moving around the sprawled bodies, he started for the entrance, then whirled as Crawley stirred, opened his eyes. He saw the startled look on the gunny's face, saw the lips opening to yell a warning. The barrel of the Colt moved in a blurring arc, caught the other on the side of the temple with a dull, barely audible thud. Without a moan, the gunhawk fell back, blood trickling from the cut on his head.

Straightening up, Brad walked swiftly to the entrance, peered out into the dimness. He would have to act swiftly now. Over to his right, he made out the line of horses, spotted Big Jet tethered a few yards from the others. A quick glance above him was sufficient to show that the wide overhang just outside the entrance would shield him from the view of anyone directly overhead. If there were any men posted on the far side of the narrow canyon, he would have to take his chance on them spotting him. Gliding along the sheer rock face, he approached the horses. It was the work of a few moments to slice though the length of rope to which they were tethered. Running for the big stallion, he grasped the reins, flung himself up into the saddle, then headed past the milling mounts, slapping one of them viciously on the rump with the Colt.

Spooked by his move, they turned and raced off along the canyon, throwing up a cloud of grey dust. The next moment, he was riding in the opposite direction, down from the hills, bent low over Big Jet's neck. He had almost reached the point where the trail dipped down through a wild confusion of up-rearing boulders and bottle-neck canyons when a sudden medley of shots and yells behind him informed him that his escape had been discovered.

Forcing the black stallion through the tangled brush, he spurred it on, digging in his heels. He did not trouble to hide his trail, knowing that by the time they caught their stampeding horses, he would be well away from the hills. A rifle cracked spitefully over to his right and against the ragged skyline, he made out the two dim figures some two hundred feet above him. The rifle spoke again and the bullet ricocheted off the saddlehorn, whining into the distance. Swinging up the Colt, he sent a couple of shots at the men, saw one of them fall back out of sight. The other ducked down swiftly, but shots continued to follow him down the treacherous slope. Shale moved dangerously under Big Jet's hooves and at one point, the stallion went down on to its haunches, almost pitching him from the saddle. Hanging on grimly with one hand, he straightened his legs in the stirrups, easing himself forward to lessen the burden on the horse. They hit the bottom of the slope in a crowd of small stones and for a moment he thought the animal was going to go over the lip of the steep drop-off, sending them both crashing to mangled ruin on the rocks hundreds of feet below.

But somehow, Big Jet managed to keep his feet and, hauling sharply on the reins, he turned him along a widening trail which cut through the narrow pass in the rocks. Breathing a little easier, aware of the sweat pouring down his forehead, he straightened a little. A desultory shot still sounded from the wall of rock directly behind him, but he was out of sight of the gunmen and the slugs went wild.

Ahead of him, the trail narrowed for a space, passing between tall columns of rock. Once through them, he knew he would be on flatter ground where the wide bench of rock angled around the hillside. As he urged the mount between the rocks there was a movement of some sort off to his right and Big Jet suddenly shied up, raising his head. Brad spun in the saddle, his gun lifted. Something dark flashed down from a narrow ledge, something human in outline. The impact of the other's body, hurtling down from the rocks, struck Brad on the shoulder, knocking him clean out of the saddle. They hit the ground hard with the gunman uppermost. Twisting savagely, Brad brought a knee up into the other's groin, heard the sharp hiss of air from the killer's teeth. But although the man weighed probably thirty pounds less than Lando, there was a wiry strength in his frame and he hung on grimly, hands flicking out for Brad's throat, clamping tightly around it as he leaned forward, straddling Lando's chest with his legs.

Tightening the muscles of his neck, feeling his eyes bulging in their sockets, Brad worked his arms between the other's, exerted all of his strength in an attempt to force them apart. The other grunted with the effort he was exerting, gouging his fingers deep into Brad's windpipe, striving to throttle him. It was almost impossible to loosen that constricting hold. Brad felt the darkness come seeping out of the rocks to envelop him, knew that he had to break the hold soon or perish.

Sucking air into his chest, his temples throbbing as if an iron band had been placed around his skull, drawing inexorably tighter, he suddenly went limp. The other hesitated, only for a fraction of a second, but it was enough. Brad exploded into action. His right fist came unleashed off the ground, swinging in a short arc that connected with the point of the other's chin. The force of the blow knocked the killer sideways and, pausing only to draw in a single wheezing breath, Brad thrust up with his left leg, heaving the man off him.

But the other was still far from finished. Rolling over, the gunhawk came expertly to his feet, moving catlike, with a swiftness that took Brad by surprise. He was still only on his knees when the other came boring in once more, swinging his booted foot at Brad's head. Had the blow landed on its intended target, it would have ended the fight there and then. As it was, Brad had been anticipating a move such as this; had guessed that the other was a dirty fighter well skilled in the art of bar-room brawling.

Twisting his head, he took the force of the murderous blow on his shoulder, felt a numbing shock run down his left arm. Grinning viciously, the gunman came in again, arms swinging loosely at his sides. There was a gun in his holster but curiously, he made no attempt to go for it and finish everything that way. As he came in, Brad got his legs under his body, gave a sharp forward lurch, the crown of his skull catching the man in the pit of the stomach, just above his belt. Uttering a bleating gasp of agony, the gunhawk staggered back, ending up against the rock wall, his face contorted as he tried to straighten up, hands clasped across his belly.

Struggling to his feet, Brad advanced on him. Those men back at the outlaw camp would not be wasting any time getting on his trail and he had to finish this quickly if he was to make good his escape. His Colt had fallen somewhere among the rocks, but he still had the knives in his belt. Flicking one out, he moved towards the killer, the long blade glinting in the moonlight. He had half-expected the other to go for his gun, knowing that there could be only one outcome of this battle now. Instead, the other lifted his hands high over his head as if in surrender.

While Brad hesitated, unwilling to kill in cold blood, even though the other would have unhesitatingly done so had the positions been reversed, the man grabbed for one of the heavy rocks balanced on a ledge just above his head. Forcing himself back on balance, the other lunged forward, bringing the boulder down with a savage force. In that split second, Brad realized that even if the knife found a spot where life lived very close to the surface, the other's downward thrust would inevitably bring that rock on top of him. There was only one move open to him. Lowering the knife, he hurled himself sideways, dropping to one knee as he did so. With a wild cry, unable to halt himself, the other stumbled over Brad's shoulder, falling forward. A thin wailing yell sounded in Brad's ears as he pushed himself upright and whirled sharply, the knife clenched in his fist.

There was no sign of the would-be assassin. Cautiously, he advanced towards the edge of the trail just beyond the narrow pass. Looking down, he made out the sprawled shape spread-eagled on the rocks some hundred feet below. The inert figure did not move and he knew instinctively that the fall would have been more than sufficient to break the other's neck.

Retrieving his gun, he swung back into the saddle, took off down the long slope. His first intention was to ride back to the Flying Y ranch and report what he had found, then he decided against it. There was still one burning question in his mind which had to be answered before he could see any connecting link in this maze of events. Reaching the trail across the alkali, he turned his mount and headed in the direction of Mendaro.

It was he decided, time he had a talk

with Jess Forlan. With most of Mendoza's band either killed or up here in the hills, together with Kerdy, it was just possible that he could get the other to talk without any interruptions from these killers. He could not get out of his mind the memory of that woman lying dead in the small ranch house which had been put to the torch.

8

Two Guns West

It was an hour after high noon, with the heat lying like a smothering haze over the streets, when Brad Lando dismounted in front of the livery stables in Mendaro. There were few folk abroad on the streets. Lying as it did so close to the Mexican border, the townsfolk seemed to have borrowed the custom of the siesta from their southern neighbours and only those who had urgent business were out in the full heat of the noon sun. A mangy cur loped from one piece of shade to another on the far side of the street as he paused and looked about him, then turned at a sudden movement at his back. A bewhiskered oldster had stepped out of the cool interior of the stables and was eying him with undisguised curiosity.

'You want me to stable your mount, Mister?' The other chewed incessantly on a wad of tobacco, spat a stream of brown juice into the dirt.'

'Sure. See that he's fed.' Brad turned Big Jet over to the other, then followed him inside.

'You know where I can find Jess Forlan at this time o' the day?'

The hostler rubbed his chin. 'Might be across at the saloon.' He jerked a thumb towards the Golden Ace. 'If he ain't there and you don't find him at his office along the street, can't say where he'll be.'

'Thanks.' Brad flipped a coin to the other, hitched his gunbelt a little higher about his middle, then stepped out into the blazing sun glare. He was aware of the close scrutiny he was receiving from the other, but did not turn, nor give any sign of his awareness. The feeling he had first experienced, that this was a town on edge, an uneasy place, was still strong in his mind as he angled across the street. He let his glance roam along the hitching rails, noting with satisfaction that there were relatively few horses tethered there. At least he had got here ahead of those gunhawks who had captured him, he reflected grimly. But how long he would have that advantage, he could not tell. Unless they had guessed that he might be headed this way, they could still be scouring the desert for some sign of him, knowing full well that unless they caught him quickly, he could spill the vital information he had concerning their hide-out to the wrong people.

He trudged up the street, glancing mechanically at the buildings on either side as he passed them. Here and there, a lounger in a high-backed chair in the shade of the awnings over the board-walk, regarded him as he went by, but that was all. He headed first for the other's office, tried the street door. It was locked and the dust which caked the windows made it impossible to see anything inside.

A short, fat man with a protruding stomach and a quivering double chin that overlapped the sweat-stained collar of his shirt, came hurrying along the boardwalk. He flashed Brad a quick glance, would have brushed past, had not the other put out a restraining arm.

'I'm lookin' for Jess Forlan. It's important. You know where I can find him?'

'Jess?' The man's eyes widened just a shade. He glanced about him as if he expected to see Forlan standing right behind him, then said thickly: 'Ain't seen him for more'n an hour. Last I saw, he was headed for the telegraph office.'

'Where's that?'

'Right on the edge of town. That way. You can't miss it.'

As the other had said, it was impossible to mistake the telegraph office. It stood on a patch of empty ground, more than fifty yards from any other building. Brad thrust open the door and stepped inside. The clerk glanced up from behind the desk, eyed him quizzically.

'Jess Forlan been in?' Brad asked.

The man glanced up at the clock on the wall behind him. 'He was here, but he left almost half an hour ago. The Golden Ace is the most likely place to find him about this time.' The other turned his attention back to his work, then lifted his head as Brad reached the door, called out:

'Wait a minute! Now I come to think of it, he didn't head back into town after leavin' here. He had his horse outside, rode off along the east trail.'

'You got any idea where he might have headed?'

The man shook his head dubiously. 'Knowin' Forlan, it could be anyplace. He keeps his business strictly to himself.'

'Thanks anyway.' Outside the office, Brad stared off into the sun-hazed distance. Forlan certainly appeared to be an elusive sort of character. Heading back to the stables, he reclaimed his mount and, under the puzzled stare of the groom, mounted up and rode quickly along the main street. The trail out of town soon led through rough country and there were too many tracks for him to be sure of following Forlan.

Very soon, he found himself skirting the massive buttes and mesas which lay to the side of Mendaro. Coarse scrub dotted the region and in places it was virtually impossible to follow the trail, which was little more than a scar of well-trodden earth that twisted in and out of the sandstone buttes in a bewildering manner. He was some five miles out of town when he spotted the lone rider off in the distance. He saw the man had halted his mount and was climbing up into the rocks, trailing a rifle with him. Brad guessed that he was perhaps a mile away and pulled Big Jet into the long shadow of one of the buttes so as not to be spotted.

From what he could see of the other, the man was being cautious, was watching his back trail carefully as well as scanning the terrain ahead of him, almost as though he were looking for someone — or something. He did not doubt, after what the telegraph clerk had said, that it was Jess Forlan. Beyond the line of buttes, the country was more or less open and he knew that it would be far from easy to approach the other without being seen. Yet he wanted to take this man alive if it were at all possible. There were important questions to be answered, answers which he felt that only the other could give. Whether he would without prompting was a different matter.

Circling the buttes, he came upon a stretch of ground where a deep depression had been worn into the rock by some river in long ages past. From the look of it, he reckoned that it would be possible for him to make his way along it for most of its length without being seen by anyone on the higher ground which lay some distance to his left. Putting Big Jet down into it, he progressed slowly and warily, keeping his gaze fixed on the spot where he had last seen Forlan. Just what was the other doing out here alone, he wondered? Had he arranged with Mendoza and the others to make a rendezvous at this out of the way spot, where they could talk without fear of being seen or overheard?

Easing the Colt from leather, he checked Big Jet as they came to the point where the gulch petered out, the ground lifting slightly ahead of him. From here, he would have to go forward on foot. Choosing a path through the scrub which would keep him in the lee of the low hills, he entered the narrowness of a defile, was halfway along it when a faint sound from up ahead caused him to draw back instinctively into the shadows. He studied the terrain before him thoughtfully. He was slightly lower than where he estimated Forlan's position to be and beyond those rocks in front of him, he reckoned there was a small plateau.

Crawling along through the hot rocks, keeping under cover, he edged towards the rim of a sharp spur of sandstone. Then he raised his head slowly until he was looking down towards the position where he fancied the other lay. There was still no indication that his approach had been noticed. He could see no sign of the other, but as he pulled his head down he distinctly heard the faint whinny of a horse nearby. Just a little more around to the right and a little closer, he thought tensely. Mesquite bunched thickly all around the rim of the plateau and, parting the prickly branches with his left hand, he peered through the gap.

Flat on his stomach, but with his elbows raising him enough to see over the tumbled rocks in front of him, he made out Forlan's figure some twenty yards away. The rifle lay on a rock beside the man, within easy reach of his right hand. Forlan was turning his head slowly, his hands in front of him and for a moment Brad puzzled over what the other was doing. Then he realised that he had a pair of glasses and was sweeping the surrounding terrain.

Brad waited for a few more moments, then eased himself to his feet, the Colt in his hand trained on the other's broad back. Some sixth sense seemed to warn Forlan of his danger, for he dropped the glasses and twisted sharply, his hand snaking out for the Winchester.

'Don't try it, Forlan!' Brad said sharply. 'Or I'll drill you here and now.'

He saw the other stiffen abruptly, then relax. The man turned his head to stare up at him, at the black hole of the Colt levelled on him. Then he forced a quick grin. 'I guess you're that man they call Lando,' he said easily. There was no trace of fear in his voice.

'You guess right.' Brad went forward, lifted his foot and kicked the rifle out of the other's reach. 'Now get on your feet and shuck your gunbelt.'

In reply, the other stood up and opened his coat, showing that he wore no gunbelt. There was a tell-tale bulge under his left armpit, however, which Brad noticed at once and ramming the barrel of the Colt into the other's stomach, he removed the small pistol from the shoulder holster and stuffed it into his belt.

'You're very observant and thorough, Lando.'

'When you get shot at as often as I have since I rode into Mendaro, you learn to be careful.'

'Do you mind if I lower my hands now?'

'All right. But don't try anythin',' Brad warned. 'After what happened to Dave Lawson, I won't hesitate to put a bullet into you the first wrong move you make.'

He saw the other's face change at the mention of Lawson's name, but it was not a look of guilt that flashed over his features. 'I tried to stop that shooting, but there was nothin' I could do. I'm sorry about your friend's death.'

'Not half as sorry as you will be

before I'm through.' Brad's tone was soft, dangerously soft.

'Maybe if I was to show you something, you might feel different about that.'

'I don't reckon there's anythin' you can show me that'll change my mind about that.'

'I think there is.' The other moved his hand slowly, dug into his vest pocket. When he withdrew his hand it held something that glistened in the sunlight. He held it out to Brad who took it carefully, staring down at it. *It was the badge of a United States Marshal!*

★ ★ ★

'Now you can appreciate my position here in Mendaro,' said Forlan quietly. 'Until I find out who's behind this rustlin' and killin', I can't afford to disclose my identity to anyone but you. Kerdy was out of the question from the very beginnin'. I soon discovered he was in cahoots with those half-breeds from across the border.'

'And all that talk about protectin' the small ranchers from Mendoza?'

'Bluff, most of it. The State authorities have known of the trouble brewin' here for some time now. My orders were to worm my way into the confidence of the big men in Mendaro, make it look as though I'm workin' for the same thing they are. I've been usin' a trial-and-error method, treatin' everybody as a suspect, studyin' them and tryin' to eliminate one after the other. It hasn't been easy and I'm still workin' in the dark.'

'You're sure that nobody in Mendaro suspects you?'

The other shrugged his shoulders. 'I'm sure of nothing. All I can do is keep up this front and trust to luck.'

Brad grinned. 'Maybe you won't have to wait long for somethin' to break. I've got the feelin' that whoever the hellion is that's behind all this, he'll soon find himself short of hired killers. We smashed one of Mendoza's bands the other night, left half of 'em dead in front of the Flying Y line camp.'

Forlan raised his brows a little at this piece of information. 'Now that's mighty interestin',' he conceded. 'It could mean that they'll be forced to push things too much for safety. Trouble is, unless we can find out who we can trust and who we can't, we don't have much chance of buildin' up a force to meet them when the showdown comes.'

'What were you tryin' to do when I came up on you?'

'I'd sort of figured that Mendoza might be headed this way. He pulled out of town early this morning with half a dozen men. Seemed in an all-fired hurry. I sent a wire to the marshal in Forbes City, askin' for help and information. When it arrives, I might have somethin' to go on. I know you've been on the prowl ever since you rode into Mendaro. You find anythin' at all?'

'Only that somebody has been

passin' information about the where-abouts of the Flying Y herd to Mendoza so that he knows exactly where it is and when to strike to the best advantage. I thought I'd found the critter, but it turned out I was wrong.'

'What about Callaghan. He's the biggest man in the territory right now.'

'He's a real deep one,' Brad admitted.

'He'd stand to gain a lot if all the other ranchers were put out of business. But from what I hear, he's been losin' cattle too to these rustlers.'

Brad nodded, then paused, whistled thinly through his teeth. 'Maybe we've been barkin' up the wrong tree all the time,' he said musingly. 'A few nights ago, he lost five hundred head, rustled off by these Mexes. We figured they had been driven clear across the border, but a while later, a strange thing happened.'

Forlan lifted his head, stared directly at him. 'What was that?'

'I came across that rustled herd in a small valley right on the southern edge of the Flying Y range. It was guarded by some of Mendoza's men. I thought then that it was odd they hadn't gone on over the border where they'd be safe. So I rode out to the ranch and reported it to Callaghan.'

'And — ?'

'He rode out with me that night. When we got to the valley there was no sign of those steers, but there were a couple of men in the rocks. One of 'em — I couldn't see who it was — damn near killed me.' He fingered the scar along his skull. 'When I came round, I found Callaghan bendin' over me.'

'So for all you know, it could have been Callaghan who shot at you.'

Brad twisted his lips into a wry grin. He was beginning to see things a little more clearly now and cursed himself for being such a blind fool that he had not considered this before. Everything was now beginning to slot into place, all of the scattered bits of the jigsaw falling into a recognizable picture that made sense.

'If it was Callaghan, then it explains a whole heap of things that have been puzzlin' me for a while,' he admitted. 'It means that Callaghan has been deliberately arrangin' for his own herd to be rustled so as to divert suspicion from himself. So far, he's been only too damn successful.'

'Too successful. It won't be easy to prove a damn thing against him unless we can tie him in with Mendoza.'

'Or force Mendoza to talk.'

'That won't be easy either. We're too damn close to the border here for my likin'. The first sign of trouble that they can't handle and they'll be across into Mexico before we can stop 'em.'

Brad bit his lower lip thoughtfully. 'Does Mendoza reckon that you're the big man behind all of this?'

'Not the really big man. My bet is that he's tied in with Callaghan. After what you've told me I'm sure of it.'

'But he still figures you to have an interest in these underhand deals?' Brad persisted.

'That's so,' acknowledged the other. He drew his brows down into a hard line.

'Then the chances are that he'll be headin' into Mendaro right now to report on what's happened. I'm fairly certain that few, if any, of the Flying Y crew are in on this. They just take their daily orders from Callaghan and they're as much in the dark about his true activities as I've been.'

Forlan pushed himself stiffly to his feet, trailing the Winchester in one hand. 'I think we're wasting time now,' he said quietly. 'Let's get back into town. Once we get there, you'd better stay under cover.'

'Don't worry none about me. I can take care of myself.' Brad swung up into the saddle, rode alongside the other as they headed towards Mendaro.

★ ★ ★

The long shadows of night spilled out over the small office, filled the corners with a deep gloom which the single lamp on the desk could not penetrate. Sitting within the rim of light, Jess Forlan drew the desk lamp a little nearer the far edge of the desk, raised the wick slightly to increase its glare.

Across from him, Sheriff Kerdy sat uneasily in the tall chair while Jose Mendoza lolled against the far wall near the door, a couple of his men flanking him, their eyes bright in the dimness. Getting to his feet, Forlan went over to the single window, drew the curtain aside and peered out into the street.

'You expecting someone?' asked Mendoza in a mildly deceptive tone.

Forlan gave him a hard stare as he returned to his seat. 'Obviously,' he said sourly. 'You don't think I'd be waitin' here at this time of night when I could be in the saloon, if it wasn't important, do you?'

Kerdy leaned forward in his chair, his face flushed. 'We was tellin' you about this hombre, Lando,' he said hoarsely. 'Now that he knows where the hideout is he can be more'n dangerous. He can wreck all of our plans.'

Forlan gave a tight smile. 'You worry too much, Kerdy,' he said evenly. 'Lando is nothin' more than a trail drifter. Like every other of his kind, we can buy him off if ever the need arises.'

Kerdy shook his head vehemently. 'You don't know him, Forlan. I'm tellin' you that he's not like the others. Once he gets his teeth set in somethin', he never lets go. You can't buy off a man like that.'

'Then we can always use some other means of makin' sure that he won't talk.'

'We've got to find him first, damn it. Don't you realize that all of our lives are at stake unless he's silenced? I've heard of him. There was talk around Abilene and Senorro. Don't go by his appearance. He's a killer and fast with a gun. There are more'n a score of dead men whose tombstones testify to that.'

'Maybe so. But that's no cause for us to stampede ourselves into any rush actions. We can take Lando any time we want.'

'And if we fail?'

Forlan's face assumed a hard, grim expression. 'Sometimes you can be a very tryin' man, Kerdy. I often wonder why we elected you sheriff.'

For a moment, the other looked on the point of retorting sharply to the implied insult, then he thought better of it and closed his mouth with an audible snap.

From the doorway, Mendoza said softly: 'Nevertheless, Señor Forlan — the sheriff has made a very pertinent point. If this man is as dangerous as he says, then to overlook him and let him run around loose out there for a minute longer than necessary, could be bad. Either he's back at the Flying Y spread, or he's here in town. Either way, I still have enough men here to make sure of him this time.'

Forlan eyed the other steadily for several moments before speaking, then said sharply: 'You've had plenty of chances already to finish him, yet he's still alive. What makes you so certain that you'll succeed this time?'

The other started away from the wall with a smooth, catlike movement, his hand starting down for the gun at his waist. Then he controlled himself with an obvious effort, but there was still murder in his eyes. 'Don't push me too far, *amigo*,' he warned silkily. 'I'm not like the sheriff. I do not take readily to insults.'

'Forget it, Mendoza. You know that we both need each other if we're to succeed. If we start fightin' among ourselves we really are finished.'

'You still ain't told us who we're waitin' for,' put in Kerdy. His eyes narrowed down a little as a sudden thought struck him. 'You ain't been holdin' out on us about Lando, have you? And brought in a couple of fast guns to take him off our hands.'

'No. This is different business. Let's just say that I've been askin' questions around town and come up with some answers I didn't expect.' He flicked his glance towards Mendoza as he spoke. 'I've invited a particular friend of yours, Jose. Jeb Callaghan.'

The other returned his look without so much as a blink of an eyelid. 'Why should you think he is a friend of mine?'

Forlan pressed his lips together, smoothed down some of the papers on the desk in front of him with calm, unhurried movements. 'I've been hearin' things about those Flying Y steers that have been supposed to be rustled. Seems they weren't driven across the border, after all. They was all holed up in some hidden valley on Callaghan's own land. My guess is that he arranged it all just so that nobody would suspect him of bein' implicated in this deal. After a time, of course, they were quietly pushed back into the main herd. He never lost a single head of beef at all.'

Mendoza made to speak, his face flushed, but Forlan stopped him with a wave of his hand. 'I'm not a greedy man. If Callaghan is in on our deal, then all I want is that it should be out in the open among the rest of us and not done in an underhand way like this.'

'You are a very generous man, Señor. Very well then it is true. Callaghan has been supplying us with guns and ammunition in return for our help against some of the other men in the territory. Since there was talk about every other spread bein' attacked but his, we planned to drive off some of his cattle and keep them hidden.'

Forlan's smile was a cold one. 'And kill his men. That was also part of the deal?'

'Of course. If we hadn't — '

There was the sound of heavy footsteps on the stairway outside. Mendoza glanced round quickly, said something in Spanish to his men who took up their positions on either side of the door, guns drawn. Kerdy swivelled sharply in his chair, his florid features startled. Only Forlan did not show any surprise.

'That'll be Jeb Callaghan now,' he said calmly. There came a sharp rap on the door.

'Come in, Callaghan,' Forlan called loudly.

The door was pushed open slowly and Callaghan stood framed in the doorway. He blinked his eyes against the light, then stepped through, jerking round swiftly as he became aware of the two gunmen on either side of him. Then the sudden tenseness left him and he came forward more confidently into the room. Thrusting back his chair, Kerdy rose to his feet for him to sit down.

'I got your message, Forlan,' said the rancher harshly. 'Though I don't pretend to understand it. You've got somethin' important to discuss with me. And with these men here.' He let his glance roam over the faces of the other men in the room.

'Before you go on to say anythin'

more, I think it only fair to tell you that Mendoza has told us everythin'. We know about the deal you made to supply him with rifles and ammunition on condition that he drove off the rest of the small ranchers in the territory.'

Callaghan jerked forward in his chair, his fingers gripping the edge of the desk, knuckles standing out whitely under the brown flesh with the pressure he was exerting. Then he forced himself to relax. 'So you know all that,' he said thinly. 'And what do you intend to do with the knowledge? It's my word against that of a common outlaw and killer and I know who the townsfolk will believe.'

Forlan shook his head. 'There's no question of anythin' like that,' he said quietly. 'I just wanted to get at the truth.'

Callaghan's teeth showed in a leering smile. 'Then you've got yourself a real problem. They say that when thieves fall out, honest men move in and take over

— and you're in this as deep as the rest of us.'

★ ★ ★

Crouching down on the narrow balcony outside the upper window, Brad Lando had heard and seen all that went on inside the small room. Gently, he eased the Colt from its holster, threw one last look down into the street, then thrust the window open and stepped down into the room.

'Hold it right there, *amigos*,' he said harshly, the barrel of the Colt swinging slowly to cover them all. He saw one of the Mexicans suddenly go for his gun, jerk it from leather, bringing it up in a blur of speed. Before he could press the trigger, the Colt in Brad's hand spoke authoritatively. Gunsmoke swirled about him and the roar of the explosion of the death-dealing weapon smashed within the small office. Then there was a strange, clinging silence.

Gradually, the smoke lifted, climbed

ceilingward. The gunhawk coughed painfully, sinking slowly to his knees, the gun tilting downward in his upraised hand. It clattered to the floor at his feet, skidded across the room, ending up against the wall. Sagging, the man collapsed on to his face and lay still.

Kerdy had taken a hesitant step forward, his usually florid features blanched. At the desk, Callaghan stared up at him out of narrowed eyes, his face expressionless. His mouth worked a little, but no sound came out. Then he found his voice: 'I might have guessed you were up to somethin' like this Lando. I reckon I should've shot you dead that time I had the chance.'

Brad nodded. 'That was a mistake you'll live to regret, Jeb. I must admit though, that you really had me fooled all along the line.'

'Just who are you, then? A United States Marshal?'

'Nope.' Brad shook his head slowly. 'But he is.' He inclined his head to where Forlan sat upright in his chair.

The eyes of the rest of the men followed his glance, found themselves looking into the barrel of the gun which seemed to have appeared as if by magic in the other's hand. Now it was laid unerringly on Callaghan's chest.

'You won't get away with this, either of you,' rasped the rancher. 'That shot will have been heard all over town and there are more men down there to answer to me than you can handle.'

'Trouble is, they ain't here right now and we can drop you long before they get up those stairs.'

'And what do you think will happen then? You figure you can get away from here without my men huntin' you down — and believe me, when they catch you, it will not be a quick death with a bullet. They have ways of makin' a man scream for death long before he dies.'

'Only you won't be around to see it,' Brad replied. 'And to my way of thinkin', when the Flying Y crew discover that their boss had been at the back of the murder of their companions, they won't rest until they've smashed the rest of your band, Mendoza.'

He allowed his glance to slide momentarily towards Forlan. 'I reckon we ought to take these coyotes along to the jailhouse and lock 'em all up. If any of 'em try to make a break for it, at least it'll save the town the cost of a trial and public hangin'.'

Moving around the edge of the desk Forlan whipped the others' guns from their holsters and tossed them across the room, taking care not to step into Brad's line of fire. This done, he prodded Callaghan in the back with his own weapon, heaving him to his feet. 'Let's go,' he ordered tersely.

Stepping over the body of the dead rustler, Brad motioned them towards the door, passing through it first and standing on one side as they came out, with Forlan at their backs. Callaghan flashed him a look of pure hatred as he made for the short flight of stairs. He was halfway down when a harsh voice near the street door at the bottom suddenly yelled: 'Anythin' wrong up there, Jose? We heard a shot and — '

'Lando's up here,' called Callaghan sharply, his voice rising in pitch. 'He's got a gun on us.'

Cursing savagely under his breath, Brad swung the Colt, sent shots thundering down the narrow stairs. But the man below, evidently sensing his danger, must have jerked aside, for the slug passed harmlessly through the open door. In the same instant, throwing caution to the wind, Callaghan hurled himself down the stairs, hit the bottom in a sprawling heap and rolled out into the street, yelling at the top of his voice. Brad sent a couple of rapid shots after him, but both must have missed because a moment later, he picked out the running footsteps along the boardwalk.

At precisely the same moment, taking advantage of the sudden confusion, Mendoza slashed sideways with his arm, bringing his hand down hard against Forlan's wrist. Staggering, the other fell back against the door, struggling to keep a grip on his gun. Brad halted in his run for the stairs. There was no time to go after Callaghan now, if he was to help Forlan. At the first shot, Kerdy had dashed back into the office and for a moment Brad thought that the other was intent on saving his own hide. Then the sheriff reappeared in the doorway with a Colt in his hand, swinging the barrel over the marshal.

Brad fired instinctively from the hip, the muzzle flash dazzling in the gloom. Kerdy uttered a wild, wailing cry as he took the slug full in the chest. For a moment he swayed in the doorway, then stumbled forward, his heels catching at the top of the stairs. Legs crumpling under him, he fell headlong down the stairway, arms and legs smashing against the wooden rails, splintering them under his dead weight. Hitting the bottom, he lay still, a limp pool of shadow in the lower doorway.

The second killer, although unarmed, flung himself at Brad, grabbing for the gun, pinning his arms to his sides. Savagely, with a desperate heave, Brad swung the other around, lifting him clear off his feet. The man's head struck against the wall with a sickening thud, but he still held on grimly, lips twisted back across his teeth in an animal-like snarl. A bunched fist struck Brad on the side of the head, setting his skull ringing with the force of the blow. Dazedly, he struggled to bring up the gun. The other butted him in the face with his head, reopening the wound along his temple, sending him crashing back against the rail at the top of the stairs. Grinning viciously now, the Mexican began forcing him backward, striving to force him over, one hand around his throat.

Desperately, Brad braced his legs, then lunged upward with a sudden surge that took the man completely by surprise. The grip on Brad's throat relaxed a little and he sucked air down into his heaving chest. Before the other could recover his balance, he struck out with the gun barrel. There was a soggy crunch as it caught the killer behind the left ear and with a faint bleat, he fell back against the rail, the force of the blow carrying him over.

Rubbing his bruised throat, Brad thrust himself upright. Through his blurred vision, he made out the slumped form in the doorway, ran forward and went down on one knee. Forlan had an ugly gash on his forehead, evidently caused by the sight of a gun barrel. Weakly, he staggered upright.

'He got away,' he muttered thickly, shaking his head. 'Back into the room.'

Gun in hand, Brad approached the door cautiously, then stepped inside, flinging himself to one side as he did so. But the expected slug did not come. Blinking in the lamplight, he stared about him. The office was empty, but the curtains over the windows were billowing into the room where the night breeze fanned them. Going forward, he peered warily out of the window. There was no one on the small balcony but it was not too long a drop to the ground below and there was no doubt that Mendoza too had managed to make good his escape.

★　★　★

Now, more than ever, it was necessary to get help. Two men against the bunch of killers that Mendoza could call to his aid, faced a hopeless task. The only safe axiom was to act on the assumption that Mendoza and Callaghan would waste no time in getting their men together to hunt them down. Now that Forlan's true identity was known to these men, his life was not worth a plugged nickel to Brad's way of thinking and the only help they might rely on would be the rest of the Flying Y crew. But it was essential that they should reach Flint and the rest of the men before Callaghan had the opportunity to do so.

A man as plausible as Callaghan would not find it difficult to talk these men into believing his story and even the badge and papers which Forlan carried might not be enough to convince these men of the role which Callaghan had played in that neck of the territory.

They succeeded in making their way out of town without incident, noticing that the few horses which had been tethered in front of the saloon were still there. From inside the place, there came the sound of raised voices and there were occasional silhouettes against the windows. Mendoza was undoubtedly rousing his men.

Brad was bone tired but he stayed in the saddle and followed the trail west without trouble, not even thinking about his weariness, because for him this was nothing new. They rode side by side most of the time, saying nothing, spurring their mounts over the rocky, parched ground which lay between the ranch and Mendaro. Every so often, they glanced over their shoulders, watching their back trail for the first sign of the men from town.

As they made their way down the side of the intervening range during the early hours of the morning, with the moon now clear of the eastern horizon, flooding the place with an eerie, yellow glow, they were forced to slow their pace somewhat, picking their way over the treacherous, uneven ground, eyes alert for obstacles. Here, it would be easy for a horse to put a foot wrong and throw its rider, maybe even break a leg in the innumerable gopher holes which dotted the wasteland. The moonlight too, played tricks with their vision, filling the territory with vague shadows that moved in a tantalizing manner, so that every patch of scrub seemed to conceal an enemy.

They rested their leg-weary mounts beside a small stream which ran through the low foothills some four miles from the boundary of the Flying Y spread. Stepping from the saddle as they allowed their horses to blow, Brad built himself a cigarette, smoked it slowly, feeling the chill of the night air seep through into his bones.

'You figure they're far behind us?' Forlan asked, drawing on his cigarette, the tip winking on and off redly, like a tiny fist beating against the enshrouding darkness.

'I only wish I knew what their plans are right now. Callaghan is pretty predictable. His first instinct will be to rouse the rest of his men against us, leave us out on a limb with no one to turn to. That's logical and makes more sense than anythin' else. But Mendoza is the problem. I never *expect* anythin' at all from men like that. Whatever you figure he'll do, it'll turn out to be the opposite.'

'And you reckon that it might be Mendoza who's givin' the orders and makin' the decisions in this case?'

'Could well be. If it is, then he's got

two alternatives facin' him. He can either ride with his men clear over the border and cut his losses before he loses everythin', leaving Callaghan in the lurch. Or he might try to talk the townsfolk against us, claimin' that we shot down the duly-elected sheriff in cold blood and also tried to kill the most influential rancher in the territory.'

Forlan considered that, then shrugged. 'As far as ridin' over the border, I'd say there's not a chance in hell of that. He's lost too many men in the fight with you and to a man like Mendoza, that rankles. He's got his pride to think of and if he cuts and runs like a whipped cur with his tail between his legs, he'll never live it down.'

Brad nodded thoughtfully. 'Maybe you're right. But you can't predict him. That means we've got no choice but to go on and get the Flying Y crew behind us, if we can convince 'em.'

Forlan tossed down the glowing butt of his cigarette, ground it out with his heel into the dirt. He moved back towards his waiting mount. 'Let's go then and put it to the test. If we fail, then our lives will be forfeit. It's as simple as that.'

He swung up into the saddle, waited as Brad checked the cinch. In his frock coat, he looked anything but a gunman. In fact, Brad reflected, as he mounted up, everything about the other looked out of place, apart from the grim expression on his face.

9

Death Harvest

No lights were showing in any of the shacks at the Flying Y line camp when Lando and Forlan rode up, but two armed men appeared as they reined their mounts, men who relaxed as they recognized Brad, then snapped up their rifles when they saw who rode with him.

'Relax, boys,' Brad said quietly. 'Where's Flint?'

Kernahan pushed his way forward, jerked a thumb over his shoulder. 'He rode out to check on the herd half an hour ago.' His glance flicked across to Forlan. 'What's this hombre doin', Brad? Why's he still carryin' his gun?'

'Send one of the men to fetch Flint — and hurry! Then gather the rest of the crew. There's trouble comin' — and soon.'

The other did not argue, snapped an order to his companion. Running for his mount, the other leapt up into the saddle, lashed the animal, the flying hoofs echoing over the hard ground as he spurred away in the direction of the distant herd.

Less than fifteen minutes later, he was back with the foreman and two other riders. By this time, more than fifteen men had gathered around the camp. Briefly, Brad explained all that had happened in town, saw the initial looks of disbelief on their faces turn into a hard anger at the way in which they had been used. Particularly, the callous killing of Winter hit them hard.

When he had finished, Brad turned to survey the others. 'I reckon we've been fooled all along the line,' he said loudly so that his voice carried to every man there. 'I say that we should ride into Mendaro and finish this thing once and for all. Anybody here disagree with that suggestion?'

There was no dissent. Bringing their

horses out from the small remuda, they climbed into the saddle, sat waiting; grim, angry men who saw things clearly for the first time and were determined to exact their revenge on the man who had used them in this way.

Seated alongside Brad, Flint said evenly: 'Callaghan and those men could swing back this way to see what happened to you. He's bull-headed enough for that.'

'You reckon he still has a strong enough hold over Mendoza?'

'That's the way I figure it.'

'My guess too.' Touching spurs to Big Jet's flanks, he urged the stallion out of the camp, the rest of the men falling in behind him. The few miles of grazing were soon covered and then they reached the foothills and more broken country out of which the curving range of high mountains lifted. There was little conversation as they rode; the difficulties of the trail focused all of their attention upon their mounts, for here a careless move could bring about a catastrophe.

Mile upon endless mile of the arduous journey were covered, and mid-morning found them within sight of Mendaro. The bright sun was gone now and there were dark, ominous clouds gathering to the south, with the sky holding a strange copper look. Brad threw a swift glance at it, felt a little twinge of apprehension pass through his frame. He had seen storms like this one which was fast approaching only once or twice in his life and each time they had been bad ones. Now it looked as if they were in for the grand-daddy of them all.

Forlan was staring straight ahead towards Mendaro, now less than half a mile away, a puzzled frown on his tanned features. 'It sure looks mighty peaceful, don't it?' he remarked. 'If those coyotes are still around town, my bet is that they've had men watchin' the trail. Callaghan must've realized what we aimed to do once he found we were no longer around.'

'Prisin' those devils out of there ain't goin' to be as easy as pullin' a cork,' Flint said soberly. 'My feelin' is that they might try to run for it if the fight goes against 'em.'

'That's my feelin' too.' Brad shifted slightly in the saddle. 'My idea is this: we should split up into two groups, one ridin' straight in and the other cuttin' around town to take 'em from the rear.'

No one had any better suggestion to offer and Forlan, taking ten men with him, suddenly wheeled off the main trail and struck north to circle the town. The rest of them reined up near the wooden bridge that spanned the wide river, waiting while the other force got into position.

Hardly had they commenced to ride across it, than two shots rang out in quick succession. Brad ducked his head instinctively as the thin murmur of a slug whipping past his face sounded in his ears. A splinter of wood splashed from the side of the bridge close beside him.

'That's a warnin' — they got a look-out posted at this end of the street,' Flint said sharply. He touched spurs to his mount, jerking his Colt from leather as he stormed across the bridge towards the near end of the main street. Evidently the alarm had brought the rest of Mendoza's men out of their hiding places, for drifting puffs of grey smoke showed and sharp reports echoed from a cluster of small stores which bordered the street. Riding forward into the withering gunfire was now a perilous project, but so long as they remained where they were, they could be picked off at leisure.

Bending low in the saddle, Brad sent the black stallion racing across the open stretch of the bridge and into the street, bullets whistling past his ears. His heart thumped crazily against his ribs as he thumbed shots into the windows of the low buildings. Behind him, one of the Flying Y riders pitched out of the saddle with a wild cry that was lost in the gun-thunder which rose in throbbing waves.

Then the rest of them had swept through. Wheeling their mounts in the middle of the street, they dropped from their saddles and ran, doubled-up, for cover. For red moments, all was chaotic turbulence; yells, screams, gunshots and curses. Then the firing died down a little as the enemy realized they were simply wasting ammunition, were merely firing at shadows.

Worming his way along the slatted boardwalk, Brad come up alongside the Flying Y foreman. Flint lay on his side, the Colt propped in front of him, the barrel laid on the building opposite.

'They played this deal real smart,' said the other bitterly, through his clenched teeth. 'They must've split their force, too, and taken up their positions at either end of the street to cover every way in. Now we're caught in the middle.'

The sound of renewed firing came from the other end of town where the men riding with Forlan had also bumped into opposition. Brad listened to it with only part of his mind, the rest of his attention riveted on the southern horizon. He caught at the foreman's arm, pointed without lifting his arm above the level of the rail.

The dense black clouds were piling in confusion across the sky now, bringing a half-darkness over the scene, almost as if night was coming on eight hours early. As yet, there was scarcely a breath of air in the small town and this made the spectacle of the approaching storm all the more frightening. Then, above the sound of gunfire, there came another noise, like the rumble of a locomotive, bearing down on them with a savage, relentless fury that nothing could halt.

'It's a twister!' Flint said, and there was awe and a trace of fear in his voice. 'And the damn thing's headin' this way.'

'How long before it hits?'

'Can't say. These damn storms are

always unpredictable. It could turn and veer away within seconds. Or it could keep on comin'. If it does, I reckon it'll hit the town in less than ten minutes.'

A volley of gunfire from across the street put an end to any conversation. The wooden rail just above Brad's head, shivered and vibrated strongly as leaden slugs smashed into it. Splinters of wood settled over his prone body. Snapping his Colt upwards he loosed off a string of lightning shots that were blended into a single roll of sound. Windows were smashed inward and somewhere inside the building, perhaps midway between the window and the wall, a wailing yell went up as at least one of his bullets found its mark.

The rest of the Flying Y crew had joined in the gunfire and the front door of the building literally disintegrated in the face of the leaden onslaught. Two or three bullets droned across the street and Brad, keeping low, quickly pulled himself away from the post, edging towards the nearby doorway, motioning

Flint after him. The other had already seen the danger that swooped down on them from the heavens. The thunder of the tornado was now swiftly rising to an ear-splitting roar. Dust, sucked up from the badlands over which it had passed, rose to join the funnel-shaped cloud. A roaring giant stalked the land, striding relentlessly towards the town.

Seconds later, rain and dust hit the town in a solid wave, blotting out everything in an impenetrable wall. Lesser sounds were utterly obliterated by the cavernous fury of the wind.

All thought of the men across the street was forgotten now in a fight for survival. Reaching out, pressing his body close against the wooden floor of the building, Brad gripped the door posts with both hands and held on grimly. There was nothing he could do now, but struggle to maintain his grip, no chance or time in which to get further under cover. Even to have moved further into the building might prove suicidal. Lying there, head thrust forward, every muscle and fibre in his body stretched to breaking point, he tried to force air down into his gasping mouth. The upward pull of that swirling funnel of wind, tearing around at unbelievable velocities, was incredible.

He heard the protesting shriek of timber, torn from its foundations, splinter and crack like so much matchwood. Tremendous crashes boomed along the entire length of the street as walls bulged outward, roofs collapsing with booming explosions. Whole pieces of warped board went sailing along the street, smashing down the rails along the boardwalks. Somewhere in the distance, a horse neighed shrilly in mortal terror. Thunder raked across the berserk heavens, tearing the clouds apart with lancing fingers of lightning.

Brad's arms felt as if they were being dragged from their sockets. With an effort, he lifted his head as a rasping screech close at hand sounded above the roar of the tornado. The building across the street teetered precariously as if a giant hand were thrusting up at it, rocking it on its very foundations. He glimpsed the white faces of the men at the windows through the swirling cloud of rain. Then the bullet-spattered door burst off its hinges, went spinning along the street. A moment later, two men staggered out into the open, running forward, their arms and legs flailing helplessly.

He blinked his eyes as tears and scouring dust threatened to blind him, unable to tear his gaze away from the scene of utter destruction. God, what blind, stupid fools! They didn't stand a chance like that. Even as the thought flashed across his numbed mind, a careening plank, sweeping along the street, smashed into one of the men, pitched him several yards, his back broken under the bone-shuddering impact. His companion slithered to a halt, terror written all over his contorted features.

Then, in front of Brad's incredulous

gaze, he saw the man lifted into the air, a puppet-like figure, jerked with invisible strings. Carried more than twenty yards by the gigantic force of the wind, the stricken gunman was hurled against the roof of the livery stables, pinned there for several moments, his body limp and slack before the savagely harrying wind abruptly released its hold on him and he toppled into the street below, a huddled, broken thing in the open doorway.

As swiftly as it had arisen, the full fury of the storm was beginning to diminish. It was becoming easier to breathe again. Weakly, Brad allowed his stiff fingers to release their hold on the canted door post. The rain still slashed down against his face, running into his eyes, plastering his hair close against his scalp. Beside him, Flint groaned, rolled over and tried to get to his feet, but Brad put out a restraining arm and held him down.

They lay quite still for several minutes, waiting for some of the strength and feeling to return to their numbed, bruised bodies. Slowly, the tremendous thunder of the tornado was receding into the distance. Rubbing his eyes, he felt the grit which had worked its way beneath the lids, grate against his eyeballs, stinging like fire. It was a while before he was able to see clearly and his throat felt as if it had been abraded with sandpaper. Every breath he took sent a spike of agony burning through his chest.

Pushing himself stiffly on to his elbows, he peered about him. The light was getting stronger now, the sun beginning to show through the rapidly thinning cloud. All about him lay a scene of desolation. The twister had blazed a narrow path of savage fury at an angle across the town, flattening buildings, leaving a trail of carnage like a swathe cut through corn. Most of the buildings at the far end of town were, he noticed, still standing, virtually unscathed. But close at hand the destruction had been almost complete.

Wreckage lay everywhere with huge planks and sections of timber piled one on top of the other as if flung there by a wilful child. Grunting, he got to his feet, held on to the side of the building, now canted at a precarious angle, feeling it shake under his touch as he fought to steady himself.

Flint staggered upright, brushing himself down. Dirt plastered his wet clothing and there were narrow, bloody weals across his face and hands. Brad knew that his own physical condition was little better. But they had been lucky. The short row of buildings in which Mendoza's men had secreted themselves had been virtually smashed to the ground. Picking up his gun from where it had fallen, he moved slowly across the debris-littered street. Several other men were emerging from where they had thrown themselves.

Cautiously, he approached the wrecked stores. There was still the chance that some of the enemy were still alive, might still be potentially dangerous. For a moment, he wondered if Callaghan and Mendoza had been in these buildings when the storm had struck. Treading warily, he picked his way among the twisted timbers, eyes alert, the barrel of the Colt pointed straight in front of him, his finger tight on the trigger.

'Can't be any of 'em still alive in this mess,' muttered Flint, his voice strangely loud in the incredible silence that now lay over everything.

Scarcely had he spoken than twin spits of flame came out of the rubble at the rear of the smashed building. One of the Flying Y men dropped, clutching at his chest. Brad stumbled over his body as another shot rang out. A dim shape rose up from the rubble. Brad had a fragmentary glimpse of the bloody mask beneath the dust-smeared hat. Then he caught the other around the middle and they went down together with the Mex on top. The other twisted violently and Brad felt the claw-like hands reach out and grip him savagely around the throat. Jerking his head back, he slammed down with the barrel of the Colt, heard the sickening crunch of steel against flesh and bone. The other uttered a thin exhalation of breath, then sagged limply, his head dropping back on to the planks.

Staggering to his feet, he stumbled on, ordering the men to search every place for any of the killers who might still be alive. Boards creaked and swayed dangerously under their feet and threatened to pitch them on to their faces as they scouted the ruins. One wall, at the very back, fronting a narrow alley, was still, miraculously, standing. Approaching, he thought he heard a faint moan and a second later, saw an arm protruding from the fallen boards. Reaching down, he grasped them with both hands and pulled them back, exerting all his strength.

Gradually, the limp body of one of the men came into view. Flint moved across at his shout, hauled the remaining debris off the man. Going down on his knee, Brad turned him over. It was Mendoza. The Mexican was badly injured. There was blood streaming from a deep cut along his forehead and the gasping cough was an indication that his chest had been crushed by the massive weight of the wall as it had toppled on him.

'Help me get him out of here,' Brad commanded tightly. 'Maybe he'll live to face a jury.'

The foreman shook his head sombrely. 'Not a chance.' He indicated the spreading red stain on the front of the other's shirt. 'He's been lung-shot too by the look of it.'

The other's eyes flicked open, stared up into Brad's. For a moment, they were filled with a malignant hatred, then the expression died slowly and Brad guessed that Mendoza must have suddenly realized just how close the end was for him.

'You're finished, Mendoza,' he said softly. 'Where's Callaghan? Was he here with you?'

For a moment, he thought the other had not heard him. Mendoza was seized by a violent fit of coughing and a thin trickle of blood spilled from the corner of his mouth and dribbled down his chin.

'You may as well tell us,' Brad persisted. 'We're goin' to get him, wherever he's hidin'. And for what it's worth, you won't end up on the end of a rope.'

The Mexican's lips worked for several moments before any sound came out and Brad had to bend close to make out the words. 'He's . . . he's with the others . . . at the far end of town.'

A grating rattle came from the other's throat, then his head fell back and he lay still.

Straightening up, Brad turned to the rest of the men. 'You heard what he said. There's nothin' more we can do here. Let's get down there and help the rest of the boys.'

A few of the townsfolk were coming out and surveying the damage as Brad and the Flying Y crew ran along the street, forced to climb over piles of wreckage where the remains of buildings completely blocked the street. As they ran, they picked out the steady rattle of gunfire. Evidently Jeb Callaghan and the rest of his cronies were still holding out.

Here, the storm had done comparatively little damage. Most of the buildings were still standing although several doors and windows had been blown in by the force of the wind.

Brad spotted Forlan crouched down in the mouth of a narrow alley and ran over. Shafts of flame split the gloom inside the buildings and bullets hummed dangerously close as he raced for cover. Little puffs of dust spurted up around his feet and something plucked at his sleeve in the split second before he dived for the edge of the boardwalk steps.

'We've got 'em pinned down inside the saloon yonder,' said Forlan tightly. He looked about him as the rest of the men ran for cover. 'We figured most of you were goners when we saw that tornado hit.'

'Mendoza and the others came off worse than we did,' Brad replied thinly. 'He's dead and most of his men. Before he died, he told us that Callaghan is holed up with this bunch here.'

'He's in there all right. What's the next move?'

Brad pointed towards the saloon with his gun. 'We've got to rush 'em,' he said. 'Risky, of course, but it's the only way.'

Bunching together as much out of sight as possible, they ran at an angle across the street, up on to the narrow boardwalk, throwing themselves flat as defensive gunfire crashed out from the windows. The air was filled with the acrid stench of gun smoke, stinging the back of their nostrils.

While a group of men moved around to the rear of the saloon, Brad and the others edged towards the gaping doors. A flurry of gunfire came whistling through the opening and then Brad had flung himself through, diving for the floor. More of the Flying Y crew came in after him, firing as they came.

Prone on the floor, Brad jerked up the weapon in his hand, saw a blur of movement near the bar and fired instinctively. The man uttered a shrill yell, whirled, the gun in his hand belching flame and smoke. A thin sliver of wood, gouged out of the floorboards, struck Brad on the neck, drawing blood. Then he fired a second time, saw the man reel drunkenly, throwing his gun away as though it were alive. For a couple of seconds, the killer hung against the bar, then put out his hands, blindly, as if to prop himself up, before falling on to his face in the sawdust.

Scrambling upright, Brad ran forward. From behind overturned tables, the remaining survivors were firing into the mass of men spilling in through the shattered doors. Desperately, Brad cast about him for some sign of Callaghan. Knowing the other, the crooked rancher would leave these men to take care of themselves while he made good his escape.

Leaping for the stairs that led to the upper floor, he took them two at a time. Halfway up, there came the booming report of a handgun from directly above him, the bullet fanning his cheek.

Dropping to his knees, he fired into the gloom of the long passageway that opened out at the top of the stairs. Above the racketing din, he thought he heard the other cry out, but it was impossible to be sure. Pressing himself close in to the side of the stairway, he edged up an inch at a time, straining to pick out the slightest sound from above.

He was almost at the top when he heard Callaghan's voice. 'I'm finished, Lando. I'm givin' myself up.'

'All right. Throw down your gun and come on down with your hands lifted.'

A pause, then a Colt came clattering out of the dimness, hit the top of the stairs and bounced down to the bottom.

When there was no further movement, Brad called again: 'I said to come out with your hands up.'

'I can't, damnit! You got me through the leg.'

Brad's finger tightened on the trigger, then relaxed slightly. Alert for a trick, he began to mount the remaining stairs, peering into the long shadows, trying to estimate where the other was.

'Hell! I've thrown down my gun. What more do you want? I'm bleedin' to death here. I need a doctor.'

Cautiously, he lifted his head, drew it down swiftly as gun-flame blossomed crimson-blue near the far end of the corridor. Thinning his teeth, he swung the Colt around, sent two shots ripping into the dimness. So it had been a trick, after all.

There came the sudden thud of a falling body. In the faint light, he made out the limp arm protruding from a doorway. Cautiously, he advanced on the other, lowering the barrel of the Colt to cover the man. But there was no further need for caution. Jeb Callaghan had played his last card off the bottom of the pack. The bullets had taken him full in the chest, killing him instantly.

Thrusting the Colt back into its holster, Brad made his way slowly back down the stairs. The fight in the saloon was finished now, the last of the survivors being led out into the street by the grim-faced Flying Y crew. Stepping through the doorway, he drew in a deep breath, looked about him. There would be a lot of rebuilding to do in Mendaro, he reflected as he stared at the scene of carnage; but with these men dead or brought to trial, the chances were that it might be a better place in which to live.

THE END

We do hope that you have enjoyed reading this large print book.

Did you know that all of our titles are available for purchase?

We publish a wide range of high quality large print books including:
Romances, Mysteries, Classics General Fiction Non Fiction and Westerns

Special interest titles available in large print are:
The Little Oxford Dictionary Music Book, Song Book Hymn Book, Service Book

Also available from us courtesy of Oxford University Press:
Young Readers' Dictionary (large print edition) Young Readers' Thesaurus (large print edition)

For further information or a free brochure, please contact us at:
Ulverscroft Large Print Books Ltd., The Green, Bradgate Road, Anstey, Leicester, LE7 7FU, England. Tel: (00 44) **0116 236 4325 Fax:** (00 44) **0116 234 0205**

Ħ1

112 2/12
PWC

Other titles in the
Linford Western Library:

MIDNIGHT LYNCHING

Terry Murphy

When Ruby Malone's husband is lynched by a sheriff's posse, Wells Fargo investigator Asa Harker goes after the beautiful widow expecting her to lead him to the vast sum of money stolen from his company. But Ruby has gone on the outlaw trail with the handsome, young Ben Whitman. Worse still, Harker finds he must deal with a crooked sheriff. Without help, it looks as if he will not only fail to recover the stolen money but also lose his life into the bargain.